*A
Harlequin
Romance*

OTHER
Harlequin Romances

by IRIS DANBURY

THE WINDMILL OF KALAKOS

by

IRIS DANBURY

Harlequin Books

TORONTO • LONDON • NEW YORK • AMSTERDAM • SYDNEY • WINNIPEG

Original hardcover edition published in 1976
by Mills & Boon Limited

ISBN 0-373-02011-2

Harlequin edition published October 1976

Printed in U.S.A.

CHAPTER ONE

It was not an auspicious beginning to a new job, thought Jacynth. She had just arrived at Athens only to find that she had missed the connecting plane to Rhodes. As she moved away from the information desk a young man at her elbow queried, "Did they tell you the time of the next plane to Rhodes?"

"Yes. Eight-thirty tomorrow morning."

"Good heavens!" he exclaimed, glancing at his watch. "That's a wait of nearly nine hours. It's barely midnight yet. Well, I don't fancy spending all that time here in the airport. Are you English?"

"Yes."

"Then let's introduce ourselves. I'm Raymond Gurney, known as Ray to my friends. I noticed you on the plane from London. You sat just in front of me, so that makes us fellow-passengers."

When Jacynth made no reply, he continued, "How about joining up with me and we'll go into Athens for a meal and while away some of the long night."

Jacynth shook her head. She had heard about men – or women, for that matter – who scraped acquaintance with girls at airports and hustled them off with the promise of dazzling jobs and prospects, jobs that often turned out to be very dubious indeed. Certainly the young man looked English enough, with pleasant features, blue eyes and mid-brown hair.

"I'm sorry, Mr. Gurney," she said gently, "but I think I'd better wait here. Besides, won't most of the restaurants be closed by now?"

Mr. Gurney frowned. "Closed? Not for hours yet. I've been to Athens before and I know places – quite respectable ones – that keep open much later than this."

She picked up her overnight bag and half turned away. "Sorry," she said, with a smile, and began to walk away.

"I can see that you're not too keen on going off to the city with a complete stranger." He had caught up with her in a matter of seconds. "But I assure you that I'll take care of you and bring you back here in time for the plane. After all, I want to catch it myself." He fumbled in his jacket pocket. "Look, here's my passport. I live in Bristol with my parents and I work for a firm of importers. I'm on a business trip to Rhodes."

"So am I," Jacynth returned crisply. "I'm already delayed and it's very important for me to arrive in Rhodes as soon as possible. I couldn't risk losing the first available flight."

Raymond Gurney shrugged. "Oh, well then, we'd better stay here for this interminable wait."

"But I'm not stopping you from going into Athens," she protested, "or indeed anywhere else."

He laughed amiably. "One of the nicest brush-offs I've ever received! But I couldn't go away and leave you here alone at the mercy of any roving eye that comes along."

She laughed in spite of herself. "Roving eye!" she echoed. "What would you call yours?"

"Doesn't apply to me. We're compatriots in a foreign land. Of course I couldn't leave you."

He was certainly persistent, she thought. The prospect of dozing on settees in the airport lounge was not inviting and an English-speaking companion might make the long hours of the night pass more quickly.

"Well, don't blame me if you regret not going into Athens for a more lively time."

"I'm sure I shan't find the time hang heavily," he assured her with an appreciative look at the girl in front of him. Medium height, blonde hair tied back with a ribbon, candid blue eyes and the fine, smooth skin that proclaimed her English nationality.

"You still haven't told me your name," he reminded her.

"Miss Rowan. Jacynth Rowan."

He grinned. "Actually I saw the label on your bag, but I wanted you to tell me. Shall we see if the restaurant here can offer anything?"

Dinner had been served on the plane from London, but Jacynth remembered how long it would be before the next meal and accompanied Mr. Gurney towards the bar.

"Coffee?" he queried. "Or do you prefer something else?"

"No. Coffee, please." She moved along the counter and selected a couple of cakes.

When he brought the coffees and sat down at a small table he said, "You're on a business trip, you said. In Rhodes?"

"Yes. I've been sent on a special job for one of the directors of the London firm I work for."

"Oh? Sounds interesting. What sort of line? Hotels? Property?"

"Something of the sort," she murmured evasively. She thought it indiscreet to divulge too much information to this casual stranger, however honest he might be. In fact, she was still quite vague as to the exact nature of the job she had accepted. All she had been told was that Mr. Mallory Brendon needed a secretary immediately. Her chief had warned her, "Mr. Brendon isn't a particularly easy man to work for, but I'm sure that you, Miss Rowan, will be able to cope. I understand that the island of Rhodes is delightful, especially during the spring and summer, and you should be able to enjoy yourself there when you have free time."

Jacynth had hesitated, although the chance to go abroad for a few months was tempting. At that time, she had strong reasons for wanting to stay in London.

"And what brings you on business to Rhodes?" she asked now of her companion. "Or is it hush-hush?"

"Oh, my firm is a small one. They import all kinds of fancy goods. Pottery, rugs, embroidered articles – all that kind of thing from Greece generally. Different goods from other countries, of course."

"And you travel around selecting and buying?"

He smiled in a deprecating way. "Oh, I don't do all the

7

Continent. My seniors do most of that, but I've been sent on a second trip to Greece. The first time I came because one of the directors was ill and it seems that I was not too much of a flop, so they've let me come again."

"Do you visit other islands apart from Rhodes as well as the mainland?"

"Crete, Corfu and some of the smaller ones."

He told her about some of the interesting places he had visited. "I haven't had time usually to go to the excavations and see the antiquities, except the Acropolis in Athens."

"Yes, I would love to roam around that part," she murmured.

"You should have insisted on staying several days in Athens before going over to Rhodes."

She laughed. "In my firm we don't usually *insist*. Plans are made and we fall in with them."

The hours passed and after more coffees to ward off sleepiness, Jacynth and her new friend returned to the airport lounge in search of comfortable settees.

"If you'd like to stretch out and doze off," Mr. Gurney suggested, "I'll be here all the time."

"Thank you, Mr. Gurney. I do feel rather sleepy now."

"Please call me Ray – not this formal 'Mr.'."

"All right, then. Good night, Ray."

"I'll wake you in time for the next plane. Don't worry."

She made a pillow of her fur jacket and was almost immediately asleep. It seemed only a few minutes when someone was rousing her and a voice said, "Wake up, Jacynth. We must check in soon, but we've time for breakfast first."

She struggled to a sitting position and glanced at her watch. Nearly eight o'clock. She went to the washroom and freshened herself before rejoining Ray, who had already secured some rolls and butter and steaming coffee.

"Give me your air ticket and I'll go and get our boarding cards," he suggested.

In a few moments he was rushing towards her. "Quick! Finish your coffee! We're at the wrong airport."

8

"Wrong airport?" she echoed.

"Yes. This is the international one. Our plane goes from the domestic one. Stupid of me to forget that."

She swallowed the hot coffee, nearly choking herself. "But what about our luggage?" she asked, as she followed him outside.

"That's all right. They'd take that over there already. Got everything?"

She nodded as she entered the taxi. "I'm sorry about this, Jacynth."

"All I hope is that we don't lose that plane," she muttered.

"Oh, we shall be in time, don't worry," Ray said airily.

But that was a false prophecy, for by the time they had secured their boarding cards and gone through passport control, the eight-thirty plane for Rhodes was already moving along the runway.

Jacynth stared at the plane, appalled. "It's gone!" she said inanely.

"Oh, dear! That's torn it," was Ray's comment.

"Well, what time is the next? Don't tell me I've got to wait another day." She knew she spoke sharply, but she was near to tears, blaming herself for such careless mismanagement.

"I'll find out."

The next was at midday. "Then I must make sure I'm on it," she said decisively. "It may not matter what time you arrive, but I'm expected to be punctual, although it wasn't my fault that last night's flight was upset."

She curbed the impulse to blame him. After all, he said he had flown before to the island and he could have remembered about the change of airport.

So it was late afternoon when eventually Jacynth touched down at Rhodes.

"Have you far to go?" asked Ray, by now a very subdued young man, anxious to atone for his earlier mistakes.

"I have the address," she told him. "Goodbye, Mr. Gurney. Thank you for your – company."

He grinned in a crestfallen way. "Sorry I upset your plans

in the end. Perhaps we shall meet again in Rhodes? Here's the name of my hotel and telephone number." He handed her a slip of paper. "Anyway, I wish you good luck in your new job. Hope it comes up to your wildest dreams."

She gave him a conventional smile and waved as the taxi took her out of sight of his slightly worried face. She was more than worried, too. Here she was arriving practically a whole day later than scheduled, there had been further unforeseen delay in tracing her suitcases which had arrived on the earlier plane and been stacked in some obscure corner, and now the taxi-driver was unsure of her destination.

"Kalakos?" he yelled over his shoulder. "Near the sea?"

"I've no idea," she replied, but his English was limited and she repeated slowly, "I do not know." Then it occurred to her to rummage in her handbag for the Greek phrase book and eventually she found the words, "*then ksero*" – I don't know. But that hardly advanced anyone any further.

"First time here," she told him, hoping he would at least understand that she could not help him.

He drove slowly along a coast road. Large modern hotels with swimming pools had sprung up in recent years on the fringe of the town of Rhodes. In between were small square houses, remnants of the villages which had been swept away.

"Kalakos is village?" the driver asked again.

"No. I think a large house. A villa."

He grunted and drove on, eventually stopping at a café to ask directions. Finally he pulled up outside a small gate set in massive iron railings that apparently enclosed a garden.

"Villa Kalakos," he said as he unloaded her suitcases, pushed open the gate and carried the luggage up to the house. She paid the fare, added a reasonable tip and waited on the wide stone steps of the villa under a massive pillared porch.

A knocker shaped like a woman's hand ornamented the heavy wooden door and Jacynth rapped several times. Surely she had come to the right address after all? She walked round the side of the villa to the back and shouted, "Hallo, there!" An emaciated-looking tabby cat shot out of the bushes and streaked across the path. Suddenly a woman opened a window and peered out, shook her fist at Jacynth, evidently telling her to go away.

"But I'm expected. My name is Rowan – Miss Rowan. I'm from England."

The woman shrugged and snapped the window shut.

Jacynth stood for a moment completely nonplussed. This was a fine reception! She returned to the front door. Perhaps the woman thought she was an intruder, trying to steal something.

Now Jacynth found a large black knob at the side of the front door and two or three strong pulls sent a reverberating clangour through the house. A man opened the door and Jacynth walked in quickly before he could shut the door in her face.

She repeated again her name, then thought to add that she had come to work for Mr. Mallory Brendon. Although most of her sentence was apparently unintelligible to the man, the name "Mallory Brendon" evidently registered.

He indicated that she should wait in a small side room off the spacious hall. Jacynth imagined that he had gone to tell Mr. Brendon that she had arrived, but after half an hour nothing happened.

She glanced around the room, furnished in ornate Italian style, cluttered with tables and chairs, a couple of small settees, footstools, table lamps and vases, a bureau-bookcase and an empty birdcage.

Once or twice she peered out into the hall where savoury smells of cooking tantalised her, for she had eaten very little during the day and was now extremely hungry.

How much longer was she to be kept waiting? If only someone would give her some food! At six o'clock she decided to find the kitchen where possibly the man and woman she had seen might be preparing a meal.

As she reached the door, it was thrust open and a tall man entered.

"Who are you?" he asked in English.

"I'm Jacynth Rowan."

"And what are you doing here?"

"Waiting for you, I think, if you're Mr. Brendon. I've just arrived from London."

"From the Palmerston company?"

"Yes."

"But, dammit, you're the wrong girl. I specially asked for Miss Osborn and – "

"Miss Osborn was married a few weeks ago," she told him.

"Well, what difference does that make?" he demanded.

"Only that she's gone with her husband to Canada."

"I see."

Jacynth could not restrain the small spurt of satisfaction when she saw that Mr. Brendon was slightly deflated by this news.

"And they sent you instead?"

"Yes. Didn't the company tell you?" she asked.

"Of course not, or I shouldn't be standing here asking questions. Well, let's have a look at you."

Jacynth withstood his scrutiny and herself had time to note his tanned face, the dark eyes and bristling eyebrows.

His lips tightened as he said, "You're not in the least suitable."

"Not suitable? But – " Jacynth almost reeled under this blow.

"How old are you?"

"Twenty. Nearly twenty-one. I assure you, Mr. Brendon, that I'm reasonably capable and efficient."

"Know any Greek?"

"No."

"That's another drawback," he muttered.

She wondered what other drawbacks he had already found in her.

"I'm sorry about that, but I didn't know I was coming here until a few days ago."

"And you were expected last night. What happened to you?"

"The London plane was late and the connection to Rhodes had already left," she explained. "So I spent the night in the airport and this morning we didn't realise that we had to fly from a different – "

"We? Who accompanied you?"

Jacynth flushed. "There was a young Englishman who was also coming here and – "

"So you picked up some casual companion in a foreign airport."

His mouth had set into a thin, disgusted line.

"He was only someone to talk to," she muttered.

Now he took several strides about the room, although his progress was limited by the cluttered furniture.

"Unsuitable, indeed! I suppose it's what one must expect nowadays from all you girls. All you think of is pleasure."

He had not even had the courtesy to ask her to sit down and now she fumbled for the nearest chair and sank into it.

"I've not had much pleasure today," she said in what she thought was a reasonable tone of voice. "I'm tired – and hungry, and if I don't soon have something to eat, I shall faint."

For a fleeting moment his dark eyes held a flash of sympathy, but his brusque manner soon returned. "For heaven's sake don't start fainting here. Are you delicate and subject to these fainting fits?"

"No. I'm strong as a horse." She could not keep out the sarcasm in her voice. "But even horses need to eat sometimes."

Perhaps it was her fancy or she was already lightheaded, but was there the ghost of a smile around his mouth?

"I'll see that you have a meal at once."

She longed to be shown to her room and have a chance to wash and tidy herself, but if she suggested the idea, this over-bearing man would immediately assume that she was not as hungry as she pretended.

"You'd better follow me," he said. As he held the door open for her she stumbled slightly and knocked against a small table. A vase with dried grasses went flying, although she tried to save it.

Aware that her face had gone scarlet, she mumbled an apology.

"No matter," he snapped. He paused to pick up the vase, which was not broken, although the grasses had scattered over the carpet.

He now showed her into a small sitting room on the other side of the hall. "I'll send Caterina to you." He shut the door and again she was alone. In a few moments the woman she had already seen came in with a cloth and cutlery and proceeded to lay a table. She did not speak, but regarded Jacynth with dark, sullen looks.

Eventually she brought a bowl of soup, followed by a dish of meat and vegetables, and afterwards cheese and fruit. The girl hardly cared what she was eating as long as it satisfied those awful pangs of hunger.

When Caterina came in to clear the table she beckoned to Jacynth to follow her upstairs. Jacynth was now shown into a well-furnished bedroom with a large double bed covered with a dark blue quilt.

Caterina indicated the bathroom next door, then disappeared.

Jacynth sank on to the bed in sheer exhaustion and frustration. What a welcome! True, she had arrived almost a day late and Mr. Brendon had been expecting someone else. But need he have behaved in so arrogant a manner at this first meeting? On the other hand, perhaps he considered it better to begin as he meant to go on.

Well, he had already put her on her mettle. If he thought she was inefficient and inadequate she would show him how mistaken he was.

She unpacked her suitcases which had been brought up and stowed her clothes in the wardrobe and chest of drawers. When she undressed, she discovered that the water in the bathroom was stone cold and she had to content herself with a wash instead of the warm, scented bath she had anticipated. The house itself seemed adequately heated for the time of year, mid-March, but perhaps Mr. Brendon was of a Spartan turn of mind and considered cold baths more healthy.

She had convinced herself that after all the turmoil of the last two days she would be unable to sleep, but as soon as her head touched the pillow, the world and her own troubles floated away from her.

She was already awake when Caterina brought her breakfast, drew back the curtains and opened the shutters. Jacynth now saw that her room had wide windows opening on to a balcony. As soon as Caterina had gone, Jacynth sprang out of bed, opened one window after some trouble with the catch and stepped out towards the stone balustrade, but the contrast in temperature between her heated bedroom and the morning air outside was enough to make her turn swiftly and hurry inside. In a split second she realised she had not entered her room soon enough, for across the space of the courtyard below, Mallory Brendon stood on the balcony of what was presumably his own bedroom. He was wearing a dark red dressing-gown, but his appearance was completely groomed, his hair smooth.

Hurriedly Jacynth closed the door and moved away from the window, aware that she was wearing only a flimsy nylon nightgown.

Her cheeks already burned as she remembered the way he had glared at her in his uncompromising manner. She resolved to be more careful in future, and put on a wrap before venturing outside, but then how was she to know that other rooms across a courtyard overlooked her own?

After her breakfast of hot rolls and butter and a sweet, spicy kind of cake, accompanied by deliciously strong coffee, she chose a dark sapphire blue jersey dress with three-quarter sleeves and a mandarin neckline. On her first morning she would give Mallory Brendon no chance to criticise her clothes or say they were unsuitable for office work. She paid careful attention to her make-up, using just enough lipstick to define her soft mouth, the merest touch of green eye-shadow, and brushed her fair, silky hair until it shone, then clipped it back with a tortoiseshell slide.

Well, she was ready for work. What now? Did she wait for Mr. Brendon to demand her presence or go down to wherever he usually worked?

She decided to venture downstairs and at the foot she saw Caterina. Jacynth managed in Greek the phrase "Where is Mr. Brendon?" and the woman pointed to a door down the hall.

Jacynth knocked timidly and heard a masculine voice call out what she supposed was Greek for "Come in".

Mallory Brendon was standing behind a massive desk near the window, so that his face was partly in shadow. All the same, Jacynth could easily read that his expression was not genial or welcoming.

"Sit down, Miss – er – " he snapped.

"Rowan. Jacynth Rowan," she supplied.

There was a long pause at the end of which he sat and half turned away from her, so that his profile was clearly outlined. The long straight nose, no hint of gentleness about the mouth, a determined chin and thick dark hair smoothed into sleekness.

"I've decided to send you back to England," he said as he opened a folder and shuffled some papers.

She half rose from her chair in protest, but subsided at a gesture from him. "Surely that's most unfair!" she exclaimed. "You don't even know – "

"Perhaps you would kindly wait until I've finished what I have to say," he interrupted. "Diana Osborn has worked for me before. She was very satisfactory – in every way." He paused, and Jacynth thought she detected the slightest hint not only of regret but of some nostalgic memory connected with Miss Osborn.

She wanted to say, "Then give me a chance to prove that I can work just as satisfactorily," but she curbed that impulse and waited for him to continue.

"As Diana is no longer available – according to you – " the glance he gave Jacynth implied that she had made up the tale about Diana Osborn's marriage, but she let it go – "then I

16

don't feel disposed to accept any kind of incompetent substitute."

When he stopped speaking, although he did not look at her, she judged that some sort of answer was expected from her.

"You have no means of knowing yet whether I'm an incompetent substitute," she said as mildly as she could, for she was aware that on this initial interview, apart from last night's meeting, her whole future of remaining in Rhodes and working for Mallory Brendon depended.

"I didn't say that you were any such thing," he retorted. "You should listen more carefully. I said I was not willing to accept such a person. What you have to prove to me is that you're not that person."

"I see. It looks as though I'm already starting under a serious handicap. I suppose, in the circumstances, it isn't possible for you to be impartial."

"Why not?" he demanded. "Are you accusing me of having already made a decision to reject you?"

"I think you are unwilling to accept me, however suitable or competent I might be. It is not my fault, Mr. Brendon, that the company asked me to come here. No doubt they thought they were doing the right thing."

His lips curled into a sardonic smile. "The right thing? For whom? For you, no doubt, if you were anxious to travel at someone else's expense. Was that your purpose?"

"Not exactly, although I admit that I very much want to travel and see something of the world."

"Then we'll see how you shape up and what sort of substitute category you fall into – competent or otherwise."

For the next half hour he plied her with questions as to the kind of work she had done in London, which department she had worked in, how much she knew of the basis of property finance as it applied to hotel-building, for Mallory Brendon was in Rhodes to arrange and supervise the financial needs of several organisations erecting new tourist hotels.

Several times he seemed to be trying to catch her out, for his queries concerned matters known only to the directors.

Eventually he stopped his catechism.

"I shall expect you to work hard for me – during the time you may be here," he told her. "My work has fallen behind very seriously. Obviously, that's why I sent to London for assistance."

"And may I know how long the – er – trial period will last?" She felt entitled to ask that. He had no justification for keeping her in the dark.

But she had misjudged his inclination to give a straightforward answer. "We shall have to wait and see," he told her, his dark eyes smouldering. "The situation depends entirely on you."

Jacynth thought otherwise. This new boss could pack her back to England whenever he chose, whatever trumpery excuse he might concoct, and she wanted to avoid that possibility for quite a long time. It was not so much a question of pride, or loss of face if she were ignominiously sent back, as the desire to be separated from her problems at home by as couple of thousand miles. Being here in Rhodes and plunged into work for a man who seemed to have all the attributes of a tyrant might leave her little time to mope over her lost dreams back in England.

"Then I'll show you where you'll be working." She was recalled by Mallory Brendon's decisive voice. "I can't stand women working in the same room with me," he declared.

She gave him a mild glance, but inwardly she was saying, No, of course not. A feminine presence in your study might distract or irritate you.

Now he conducted her to the small sitting room where last night she had been served with a meal. On a table by the window was a typewriter, stationery, folders and the usual paraphernalia of office work.

"There's a whole lot of stuff of which I need copies, so you can start as soon as you're ready. You'll find my written instructions inside each folder."

He moved towards the door, then turned. "One more thing, Miss Rowan. You were probably unaware of the layout of this house, but please try not to appear on your balcony unless you are dressed. On the rare occasions when I have visitors here they might be surprised to view you so lightly clad."

She lifted her head. "I'll remember, Mr. Brendon. Now that I know how chilly the climate is, I shan't make that mistake again."

She hoped he would take her meaning about the "chilly climate" and wondered what sort of visitors he would entertain.

When he closed the door behind him, she said aloud wrathfully, "Next time I'll wear a hat and coat. Boots, too, perhaps!"

Like a shot, he poked his head round the door again. "Did you say something? Anything else you want?"

"Nothing, thank you." This time she waited judiciously a few seconds before muttering under her breath, "Nothing except a handy – and heavy – object to hurl at you."

She opened the top folder, read the instructions in Mallory Brendon's bold handwriting and began work. Somewhere about eleven Caterina brought a pot of coffee and at one o'clock served lunch on the table in the centre of the room.

So, Jacynth reflected, this was to be both her working and eating quarters. In hesitant Greek she asked Caterina if Mr. Brendon was in the house and received a definite "No."

During the afternoon Jacynth worked steadily, though not without an occasional hitch when she found it difficult to decipher Mr. Brendon's instructions out of all the mass of crossings-out, insertions, paragraphs ringed and arrowed to be transposed.

At seven o'clock she judged that she had done a fair day's work, tidied the table and stood up, ready to go up to her bedroom and freshen herself before dinner.

Mallory Brendon strode in and glared at her. "There's no need to work overtime," he snapped. Then he added with a cynical light in his dark eyes, "Unless, of course, you're a very slow worker."

She had sat down again. "You must judge that for yourself.

I've no idea what you would call a day's work."

He was standing close by her shoulder, as he picked up and examined the work she had completed, and unaccountably her heart was thudding as she waited for his approval or otherwise. She was conscious of his nearness, of his masculine presence, and even hoped he would move slightly farther away from her so that she could recover her own detached coolness.

"H'm," he grunted from time to time. Then, as he replaced the last few sheets, he said, "Not bad. Not bad at all."

Her spirits leaped up as though he had awarded her the most extravagant praise. "But," he went on, "this is only the easy part of my work. During these last weeks I've had to knock it into shape myself. In future, you'll have to cope as best you can from my rough drafts."

Jacynth made no reply. If there was any question of "future", then she was reluctant to spoil her chances by some injudicious remark.

"Right. There'll be enough work to keep you busy for the next day or two."

At the door he threw a curt "Goodnight" over his shoulder and went out.

Jacynth let out a great gasp of indignation. Of all the men she had ever had to work for, surely this man Brendon was the worst! Pompous, vindictive, inconsiderate, he didn't deserve anyone efficient or willing. It would have served him right if she'd been a nitwit, unable to type a page free of half a dozen clumsy erasures.

Then she laughed. The nitwit would probably already have been on her way back to England, and at least she, Jacynth, was provided with further work for a couple of days.

In her bedroom she renewed her make-up and changed her dress, wearing now a patterned terylene in shades of peacock blue and acid greens. At the foot of the stairs Caterina was waiting, evidently ready to serve dinner. The Greek woman motioned to Jacynth to enter again the sitting-room-cum-office, where the centre table was already laid for one.

So evidently all her meals were to be taken solitary in this room. If Mr. Brendon took his alone in the dining-room, no doubt his reason was that he couldn't stand eating in the same room as a woman!

Jacynth resigned herself to the position. After all, she had no right to demand a seat at her employer's table and if he chose to eat alone, that was surely his business. If, of course, he were alone. He might have guests, for all she knew.

She turned her attention to the book she was trying to read, but Mallory Brendon's face came between her and the printed page. Diana Osborn had worked in a different department from Jacynth's, but there had been gossip about this marvellous "man in Greece" with whom Diana had spent three or four months. At the time Jacynth had listened without much interest and she had not known the name of the man.

"Irresistible!" Diana had termed him. "The most fascinating man you could ever meet."

Obviously Mallory had wanted Diana to return, so they must have been on fairly friendly terms. More than friendly? Perhaps an affair? Diana was a very attractive girl, with beautiful features and a cloud of dark hair. Sophisticated, too, thought Jacynth, and probably knew how to handle men, even the Mallory Brendons who came her way.

Perhaps it was a jolt when he learned that Diana was married. Or was he really the heartless type who took his pleasure where he found it and cared nothing for the consequences?

For her part, Jacynth was convinced that she would find him completely resistible. Her chief concern was to stay working in Rhodes and avoid being returned to England like a wrongly-addressed parcel. Surely she could make herself as competent and efficient as Diana, so that Mallory Brendon would have no grievance on that score. As to any kind of personal relationship, that was out of the question, for she was still bruised from a recent encounter with an attractive man and her only chance of recovering was to stay out of England as long as possible.

In London she had shared a small flat with one of her own distant cousins, Sara, a glamorous fashion and advertising model, who attracted men like moths to a candle. Jacynth was often invited for a foursome at the theatre or dancing, but she usually realised that her own escort was more interested in Sara and put up with Jacynth as the necessary makeweight. Jacynth had never bothered or showed any resentment, always enjoying whatever entertainment the occasion provided. Until David came along.

He had called at the flat one evening when Sara was out with her latest admirer and Jacynth had made coffee and sandwiches. He was an architect, he told her, and had been abroad for nearly a year, so he had lost touch with Sara and her circle of friends.

Jacynth listened to him, bemused, aware only of the shattering effect he had upon her. She had to wrench her gaze from contemplation of his lean good looks, the way his chestnut hair sprang from a broad forehead, his mouth that made her wonder what his kisses would be like. She busied herself with the coffee pot, but his voice, deep and sonorous, yet with hints of laughter in its inflections, enthralled her.

When he finally left, promising to telephone Sara in a day or two, Jacynth danced around the room for sheer happiness. At last she had met the man who had captivated her from the first moment. She sobered at the thought that he was Sara's friend, but Sara had a dozen men friends and she had managed without David for almost a year.

Sara's reaction when she learned of David's visit had been perfunctory, Jacynth noted. "Oh, he's back from wherever it was. We must fix up an evening somewhere. Did he look well?"

"Marvellous," had been Jacynth's answer; she was unaware of the blissful expression on her face.

"And was he amusing?" pursued Sara.

"I could have listened to his tales for hours."

After that there were several outings of one sort or another, usually with one of Sara's innumerable acquaintances, Martin, Clive, Tony or someone else, to make up the quartet. Jacynth spent more than she could afford on new evening dresses and smart trouser suits and was delighted when sometimes David seemed to enjoy her company while Sara was occupied with the other man of the party. Dancing in his arms was very heaven and when he smiled, she was intoxicated beyond belief.

David had been back in England about a month when Jacynth was suddenly offered the chance of a few months' stay working in Rhodes. She was employed as secretary in a large property finance and management concern dealing with the erection of hotels and commercial development in many parts of the world as well as at home.

"How would you like to go, Miss Rowan?" her department chief asked her. "I'll recommend you. Think about it, but I must know by the end of the week."

She was stunned. To travel to foreign countries had been one of her keenest ambitions. Now, to be paid a handsome salary and work in fabulous places was surely a prize dropped into her lap.

But there was David. How could she leave England without knowing what his true feelings were? She had been anxious not to rush matters, but to give both him and herself time to cement a lasting affection. If she left now, David would naturally assume that she had little interest in him.

She discussed the job in Rhodes with Sara, who was all for Jacynth's acceptance.

"Chance of a lifetime, pet. Why are you hesitating?"

Jacynth wanted to say, Because I love David and if I leave now, I shall regret it all my life. Instead, she mumbled, "I'm thinking it over."

Then it was Friday afternoon and she told her chief that she had decided against the post in Rhodes.

"Pity," he commented. "I'd been hoping you were the right girl for Brendon."

The week-end was miserable, for David took Sara off to visit one of his aunts or other relatives, and Jacynth mooned about the flat in a dispirited mood.

On Sunday evening Sara returned and announced that she

was going to marry David.

The shock made Jacynth reel. "David? Not David!"

Sara's smile was gentle. "Of course David. Why not?"

"But he's – he's – " Jacynth could utter no further words and rushed away to her bedroom.

Hours later she was aware that Sara was bending over her. "Don't cry, pet," she was saying. "I know what a devastating effect he can have on any impressionable girl."

"But I love him! I love him!" moaned Jacynth.

"So do I." Sara's calm voice made the other sit up abruptly.

"You? You don't love anyone. You just amuse yourself with men. You have all the others. Why can't you – ?"

"Why can't I let you have David?" supplied Sara. "Because we love each other and I've waited a year for him. All my other men friends were just companions for an evening out and a goodnight kiss on the doorstep. Nothing else."

After a pause, Sara continued, "This job in Rhodes might be a good idea just now."

"I turned it down," Jacynth said flatly.

"What a pity! Darling, you'll see that you haven't come to the end of the world. You'll meet other men – and probably find that what you felt for David was only an infatuation."

Oh, it was easy enough for Sara to be so philosophical about the affair. She would soon be wearing David's ring and the wedding was fixed for some time in April.

"I'm sorry about that job," Sara was saying thoughtfully. "It would have been an advantage for David and me to have the flat to ourselves when we're married – until we can find something more suitable. But of course, Jacynth dear, I'm not anxious to turn you out. We shall be able to make some arrangement, no doubt."

So Jacynth's place in the flat was needed for David in due course, but in any case she could not have borne staying on there and meeting him.

On Monday morning she approached her chief and told him she had changed her mind about the job in Rhodes, if it was still open.

24

"Lucky for you, young lady, that your cousin telephoned late on Friday and asked me to hold it over the week-end. She thought you might be ready to go."

Jacynth was speechless. Anger, resentment, pride and a flash of gratitude jumbled together to deprive her of words.

"You'll have to get a move on, though," her chief informed her. "Mr. Brendon is impatient for someone to go immediately. Could you fly on Wednesday?"

She agreed. She would have gone to a remote island in the Pacific to escape the heartache that enveloped her. Although David had not encouraged her in the slightest to believe that he had a spark of love for her, except perhaps a cousinly affection because of Sara, Jacynth had not yet had time to recover from the rawness of the wound. In time she might be able to think of David as Sara's husband.

Sara's parting words at the airport had been, "Dear Jacynth, I don't mean to be cruel, but one day you may thank me for my part in hustling you abroad. Life's full of challenges and you never know what new man may be on the horizon."

Now that she was here in Rhodes, Jacynth considered that however "irresistible" some new man on her horizon might be, she was not in a condition to be attracted to him.

As for Mr. Mallory Brendon, his brusque treatment and obvious antagonism were hardly calculated to induce her to fall worshipping at his feet. She could not claim to be as attractive or glamorous as Diana Osborn, so Mallory would be quite safe where Jacynth was concerned. She was here to work and make a success of the job she had been sent to do. Nothing else.

CHAPTER TWO

JACYNTH was up early next morning, for she wanted to explore the gardens of the Villa Kalakos. So far she had not stepped outside the front door since her arrival and as yet she had no idea of the situation of the villa in relation to the town of Rhodes.

The front door was not only bolted but locked in what appeared to be a complicated manner, so she went through to where she knew the kitchen to be and met Caterina who was preparing the breakfast trays.

Caterina seemed surprised at this intrusion at so early an hour, but understood when Jacynth indicated that she wanted to go out to the garden.

"I'll have my breakfast later," she said, hoping that the woman would understand.

Outside, the morning air struck with the coolness of this time of year, mid-March, but Jacynth had prudently dressed in warm clothes and added her short fur jacket of pale musquash. Mr. Brendon need not worry this morning about her inadequate attire.

The grounds were more extensive than she had imagined, with lawns and clumps of flowering bushes, untidy gravel paths and a swimming pool, at present empty and littered with dead leaves and dust. At one end near the roadway was a windmill, but unlike any Jacynth had ever seen in Englnad. This was cylindrical, made of old grey stone and with a conical roof. A door near the ground looked as though it had not been opened for many years and the supports for the sails were in the form of an eight-pointed star.

Jacynth knew that Rhodes had been famous for its old windmills, but she had not expected to find one in a private garden.

"Interested in the windmill?" asked a voice behind her.

She turned quickly to face Mr. Brendon. "Yes. Isn't it unusual to find one here in a garden?"

"No. Every house along this part of the coast had its own mill at one time. They've not been used for many years. The grain usually goes to the mainland now to be ground."

She was about to ask him how far away was the villa from the town or if he would show her on a map, but his next words cut in sharply. "If you've finished your tour for the time being, I'd like you to come now to my study. I've some instructions."

She opened her mouth to protest that she had not yet breakfasted, but decided she had better follow him into the house.

"Sit down," he commanded. "Brought your notebook?"

"No," she admitted. Did he believe she carried it around with her on an early morning stroll?

He grunted and gave her some sheets of paper for her shorthand notes, then dictated rapidly a long report.

Occasionally a phrase was unfamiliar to her, but she would check it later rather than ask him at this moment.

Then, as though he read her thoughts, he said, "If you don't understand what I'm saying, then ask now. It causes no end of confusion if I have to switch my ideas back again."

Jacynth glanced up guiltily, and felt the swift colour flood into her cheeks, but tried to control her voice. "That last sentence – shall I read it back?"

"Naturally," he snapped. "Otherwise I can't know where you've gone wrong."

Her head shot up and she met his glance, his dark eyes like pools of challenging criticism. For a few seconds she held his glance, refusing to cringe, but when she turned her attention to her notes the shorthand outlines swam before her, blurring into nothingness and her heart thudded so loudly that she felt sure he must hear it.

She wanted to run out of the room, but now Mallory Brendon made matters worse, for, apparently impatient of her silence, he rose from his own chair and came and stood beside

27

her, looking over her shoulder at the page of shorthand squiggles. His masculine nearness made her feel weak and faint and with an effort she pulled herself together. What on earth was the matter with her?

She found the beginning of the sentence and in a slightly unsteady voice began to read.

". . . the company will make interim payments to enable the construction labour force to be paid, but detailed accounts of these payments must be rendered to the accountant so that – " She raised her head questioningly.

"So that 'spot' payments are not confused with 'forward' commitments for materials not yet essential. Got that?"

"Yes, thank you," she said.

"I see you have a problem with unruled paper. Can you manage?"

His sudden change of tone from that dictatorial bullying to a more amiable manner nearly caused her to dissolve into tears, but she swallowed hard and mumbled a reply.

He continued working for almost another hour and Jacynth was aware of her lack of breakfast. No doubt he had already eaten and assumed that she had, too. All the same, she thought, he could have asked.

Then he glanced at his watch and in a final flurry of brisk instructions he went out of the room and ostensibly left the house.

Jacynth leaned her head on her arms, sprawling across the polished teak desk. How could she go on working for such a man? Then she sat up smartly, dried her eyes and reminded herself that every new job is full of initial difficulties when one's usual routine is changed.

She found Caterina in the kitchen and asked for her coffee and rolls. The woman seemed to be concerned that Jacynth had waited so long. From a few hurried sentences, the girl gathered that Caterina had taken her breakfast up to the bedroom and left it, believing that Jacynth was only absent for a few minutes.

Later she had found the coffee pot cold and the rolls untouched. But now, without asking questions, she brewed a fresh supply of coffee and Jacynth ventured to pull a chair to the table and tackle the croissants and apricot jam, hoping that she was not infringing one of the rules of the establishment by eating in Caterina's kitchen.

For the first time, the woman smiled at Jacynth and her previous dour, unamiable mood seemed to have softened. Hesitantly, Jacynth tried out a phrase or two in Greek, but Caterina's answers confused her and she had to admit that she did not understand.

"Soon," she said, as she rose to go, "I shall teach you English."

When she returned to the room she now called in her office, she was astounded to find such piles of work awaiting her. There were notes in Mallory's bold, decisive handwriting, telling her the priorities. He must have come in before he left the house.

She worked with considerable zest for a couple of hours, fortified by the mid-morning coffee that Caterina brought. As she broke off for a few minutes Jacynth reflected that those ridiculous sensations she had experienced earlier when Mallory was dictating to her had been entirely due to her lack of breakfast. There was no other possible reason.

Somewhere about the middle of the afternoon, Caterina brought an envelope to Jacynth. It was clearly addressed to her, "Miss Jacynth Rowan, Villa Kalakos." But the writing was certainly not Mallory's. She opened the envelope and read the note inside, then gave a little exclamation of pleasure. It was from Ray Gurney, the young man with whom she had travelled to Rhodes from Athens. He asked her to meet him tonight about eight o'clock at the Café Actaeon.

The note had evidently been delivered by hand and she went out to the kitchen to ask Caterina who had brought it.

Caterina indicated that someone had given it to her husband, Nikon, when he was working in the garden.

Jacynth was puzzled over several aspects of this unexpected invitation. She supposed that Ray had seen her address on her luggage, but why did he deliver a note instead of calling at the house, or even telephoning?

Anyway, she supposed it would be in order for her to go out for the evening, although she had no idea where the Café Actaeon was situated or how far it might be from the villa. Still, she could ask Caterina for directions.

At half-past six, when she considered she had put in about a nine-hour day for Mr. Mallory Brendon, just about fifty per cent more than she would have done in any civilised office in London, she covered her typewriter, tidied the desk and hoped she had completed the correct priorities.

She had reached the foot of the main stairs when Mallory came in.

He stared at her and her cheeks burned as though she had been caught in some guilty situation like sliding down the bannisters or stealing the petty cash.

"Are you taking a rest?" he queried.

"I – I thought I'd finished for the day." She glanced pointedly at her watch.

"I'm afraid not," he snapped. "I've several urgent matters I want attended to."

He went striding into the office and Jacynth realised that she had no choice but to follow him. Perhaps he would keep her only ten minutes or so and she would still have time to go out and meet Ray.

"We work long hours here, Miss Rowan," he said when she joined him by her typewriter and uncovered it. "On the other hand, occasionally we can take a day off when matters simmer down. But that's not very often."

He implied that she need not expect much free time in the near future, and although he had said "we" can take a day off, he was certainly not offering to share it with her.

He glanced casually at some of the work she had done during the day and she watched for signs of approval or the reverse on his face. Already she was coming to know the shape of his lean features, the straight nose, firm mouth and a jawline that would defy argument. At this moment she could not see his eyes, but only the black curving brows above them. Then he turned quickly towards her and she was unprepared for that sudden gaze from his dark brown eyes. Once again, Jacynth was aware of that slightly stunned feeling when she met his glance and she turned her head sharply away.

"Right!" he said. "We'll get these new matters sorted out."

Suddenly she was angry. At least he might have said that she had worked satisfactorily! In fact, she had slaved all day, and now when she was expecting an hour or so's recreation he had to come barging in and start all over again. Quite likely the business matters were not so important that they couldn't be attended to tomorrow morning.

It was on the tip of her tongue to tell him that she had been invited out for the evening, but now it was too late. He was waiting impatiently for her to open her shorthand notebook.

More than an hour went by and Jacynth, after numerous glances at her watch, realised that her date with Ray was not going to be possible. She could telephone his hotel, but there was no telephone in this room. In fact, the only one was in Mallory's study, so she could hardly use that.

"I notice you keep looking at the time," Mallory observed, leaning back in his chair opposite her. "I suppose you want your dinner. Caterina told me that when we started work this morning, you hadn't had time to eat your breakfast. I'm sorry I kept you hungry, but I assumed that as you were strolling in the garden, you'd already breakfasted."

"Oh, it didn't matter," she assured him, relieved that he supposed it was hunger rather than a meeting with an acquaintance that made her on edge about the time. Well, it was too late now to bother about going out. Still, it would have been pleasant to talk to someone like Ray on a friendly footing.

"Well, I don't want you fainting for want of food. I don't think you'll be starved here, so tell me next time when you want to eat."

"I shan't faint," she said emphatically, "but I *am* hungry." He had invited her to tell him, so why did he now give the faintest glimmer of a smile?

31

"What a girl you are for food!" he exclaimed. "You look as though you live on fresh air and faith. Well, we'll break off now and I'll tell Caterina."

When he went out of the room Jacynth took the opportunity to slip upstairs to her room, wash her hands and face and apply fresh make-up. There was no point in changing her dress, she thought, for she was still expected to continue working after dinner. Besides, Mallory would probably only make some sarcastic remark if she went down looking as though she anticipated a social evening. She was wearing a honey-coloured silky jumper with a beige skirt, an outfit that accented her shining fair hair and the cornflower blue of her eyes.

When she returned to the sitting-room-office, she was surprised to find that Caterina had laid two places at the centre table. Jacynth had supposed that, as usual, she would be served alone, while Mallory took his meal elsewhere.

She hid a slight smile. So she was to eat in company with the great man himself. What an honour!

A few moments later Mallory came in with a bottle of wine, which he handed to Caterina who expertly drew the cork.

"Do you like our resinated wine?" Mallory asked Jacynth.

"I don't know. I've never tasted it, although I've heard of it," she added hastily to cover her ignorance.

Mallory poured a glass of pale white wine and handed it to her. "Sip it slowly in case you don't care for it."

She obeyed. The "tarry" flavour was surprising, but not unpleasant. It reminded her of roads being repaired with fresh tarmac.

"And the verdict?" he prompted

"A bit daunting at first, but no doubt one gets used to it "

As Caterina served small fish salads, his eyes appraised Jacynth across the table. "And are you easily daunted?" he asked.

She could not sustain his glance for long, for she began to feel churned up inside and now she studied her plate before answering. "It depends on the situation I'm faced with!"

32

"Perhaps we shall have to present situations to you and see how you react." His voice was challenging but more genial, and she looked across at him quickly in time to see an expression in his eyes that brought the blood rushing to her cheeks. She turned her attention swiftly to her food and began to crumble bread abstractedly.

The meal progressed with a meat dish with potatoes and aubergines covered in a browned sauce. Finally there was cheese and fruit.

Mallory told her some of the details of the hotels and other buildings being constructed in Rhodes, Crete and some of the smaller islands, and Jacynth listened eagerly, trying to remember accurately all he said. But he had now replaced the retsina wine with a light local Rhodes wine and filled her glass more than once. As she divided an orange into segments, she felt more cheerful than at any time since her arrival. Mallory – already she was thinking of him by his Christian name, even though she had to address him as "Mr. Brendon" – apparently had some vestige of a human side to his nature, and this unexpected tête-à-tête dinner was more than adequate compensation for the loss of an evening in the company of Ray Gurney.

"Whereabouts is this villa situated with regard to the town of Rhodes?" she asked. "I haven't been able to see a map yet. When I came from the airport in a taxi, I couldn't see much of the surroundings, and I haven't yet had a chance to explore."

Almost instantly his manner changed and she was quelled before he even spoke. "Oh, I can't spare you for sightseeing," he said impatiently. "I thought you understood that."

Jacynth looked away and waited a few seconds before speaking. She had imagined that while he was in this rather more cordial mood he might be inclined to give her permission for at least a few hours off duty.

Yet she was determined to stand her ground. "I didn't mean time for sightseeing," she said in an even tone. "But if I'm to have any free time at all, I should like to be able to plan it."

His dark eyebrows went up and stayed there. "Oh? And what do you intend to plan?"

"At least I might want to do a little shopping," she retorted.

"Shopping?" The way he repeated the word one would have assumed that she had announced her desire to go out gambling all night at the casino. "You girls think of nothing but how to idle away your time."

She gave him such a steely glance that he added, rather grudgingly, "Not that you've idled since you came – when you did eventually arrive."

He rose from the table and pressed a bell that evidently summoned Caterina, who came in a few moments to clear away the dishes.

"Now – where did we get to?" He had already moved to the table where Jacynth worked and she had to resume her place opposite him, but inside she was seething with fury. He had ignored the question of free time, but in such a way that she was prevented from making any arrangements. Fleetingly, she thought of Ray and wondered if he would contact her again, in view of the fact that she had not turned up tonight at the meeting place.

In London before she left she had not been warned that she might be expected to work seven days a week or that the length of a working day extended far into the evening. All right, she vowed, smouldering, if that was the way he wanted it, that was the way he would have it. When she really needed something from a shop, she would ask with elaborate politeness if he would direct her to the nearest likely place, or, better still, ask him to purchase the article for her and see how he liked being errand boy.

The corners of her mouth quivered with suppressed laughter and she bent her head over her typewriter.

"What's amusing you?" he demanded. "A few moments ago you were sulking because I refused to let you gad about the town on the pretext of shopping. Now you're smiling at some secret joke."

She coloured swiftly, appalled at the way he must have been

34

watching her facial expressions. She straightened her face into composure. "It was nothing. I didn't know I was smiling."

For an hour the two continued to work over reports and letters and estimates, but then Jacynth began to make typing mistakes through sheer tiredness. It had been a long day with an early start and now a very late finish. Apart from the lengthy number of hours, there had been these encounters with Mallory and if he were going to alternate hectoring spells with more genial interludes, then she needed to fortify herself against the contrariness of his moods.

She sighed as yet again she had to make erasures with an old-fashioned disc rubber instead of the modern correction papers.

"Yes, we'd better call it a day," came Mallory's resigned voice.

A day? she thought angrily. Only a day and a half! Did he expect her to work like this all the time? He was nothing but a bullying slave-driver and that lighthearted atmosphere between her and her employer was completely dissipated by now.

"I'll retype that page tomorrow morning," she promised coolly. "I'm too tired to see what I'm doing."

Anyone with a grain of consideration would have apologised for working her to death, but not Mallory Brendon, apparently. As she tidied away the papers and folders, covered her typewriter, she was aware of his scrutiny and she dared not look at him.

She managed to say "Goodnight, Mr. Brendon" and escape from the room before she either burst into tears of weariness or told him flatly to his face exactly what she thought of him. Neither course would probably have made the slightest difference, she reflected, as she undressed and prepared herself for bed.

The next day was Sunday and this time she was more cautious than to walk about in the garden before breakfast. In fact, she went into the office downstairs just before nine o'clock, ready to martyr herself to an unjust man.

To her surprise, on top of her typewriter was a map of the

island of Rhodes, and a street map of the city. She studied the latter, but without knowing the name of the street in which the Villa Kalakos was situated, she was still uncertain of the distance to the walled city. All she had so far discovered was that the villa was only a few yards from the seashore, but as apparently the city lay on the north-eastern point of the island, she could not be sure which coast.

She was about to take the map to Caterina and ask for directions, when Mallory came into the room. His eyes were dark and glittering, but whether with anger, irritation or some form of personal triumph, Jacynth could not be sure.

"You're free for the day, Miss Rowan," he barked. "I gather that's what you wanted, so there's no need to make a martyr of yourself."

She coloured instantly, aware of her own resolve to that end, and she saw his pointed glance at the uncovered typewriter.

"It's Sunday," he continued, "and I also have some engagements of my own."

Before she could even thank him, let alone ask for information about the map, he had slammed the door behind him.

She let out a gasp, then sank down on her chair, for her knees felt like giving way. Of all the unpredictable men! Why couldn't he have said last night that she could have the day off? But no, he had to ignore her tentative request, then hurl a day's freedom at her. Naturally, she was aware that today was Sunday, or did he imagine she was so bemused by his looks, his masterful manner that she had lost count of the days of the week?

She supposed she must be grateful for small mercies and the fact that he had provided her with a map.

Now that she was free for the day she went up to her bedroom and changed the neat office-like dress for beige trousers and a sapphire-blue shirt that enhanced the colour of her eyes. With a cream cardigan on her arm, she was ready to explore on her own, but she ventured inside the kitchen door to tell Caterina that she would be out all day and possibly she would

36

not be in to dinner in the evening. She hoped she had used the correct Greek words, but Caterina apparently understood.

Jacynth hoped to avoid meeting Mallory in the hall or outside the front door, but as she walked towards the gate, a sleek, black car glided behind her.

Mallory stopped as he drew level. "Do you want a lift? I'm going into Rhodes city."

For a moment she stared at him. He was wearing a pale fawn jacket with a cream shirt and dark maroon tie, and the prospect of sitting beside him in the car filled her with both delight and apprehension.

"I think I prefer to walk if I can find my way," she said in level tones. "Otherwise, I shall never get my bearings. I haven't yet been outside the garden."

His mouth was a taut line as he contemplated her.

"Besides," she added quickly before he could say anything to puncture her resolution, "I really think one should explore cities on foot."

"As you wish," he said curtly, "but if you lose yourself, I shan't send a search party." Was there just a hint of amusement in the relaxation of his firm mouth?

"No fear of that, Mr. Brendon," she assured him with more confidence than she possessed. "I have the map you've so kindly provided me with. I shan't get lost."

Without another word he drove forward and through the wide gates which Nikon, Caterina's husband, had just opened. Nikon smiled and wished her "*Kalimera*", to which she replied with "Good morning" in both Greek and English. He was a burly, strong-looking man with dark hair and rosy cheeks; middle-aged, but he appeared younger than his wife, who was gaunt and sallow-complexioned.

Jacynth soon realised by the direction of the sun that the Villa Kalakos was on the western side of the island point and when she saw the name of the street, she checked that with the map.

Oh, it was not very far apparently to the sharp point at the tip of the island. She walked along the railed promenade. On the opposite side a cluster of newly-built hotels faced the sea. In some cases, there were still traces of the old houses and their derelict gardens where the sites had been cleared to build the hotels. Here and there were windmills almost identical with the one in the garden of Kalakos.

When she reached the Aquarium situated on the extreme tip of the island, she paused, noting the golden beach dotted with lounge chairs and gaily-coloured umbrellas. She was surprised that they were apparently in demand so early in the year, but reflected that the temperature here in March was as warm as it would usually be in England by the end of May. Fringing the beach was a turquoise sea and far away a vague outline of land which must be part of Turkey.

As she resumed her stroll, she was wondering how she could contact Ray Gurney to apologise for not meeting him last night. She could now telephone his hotel, but he might be out. Perhaps she could leave a message. She found the slip of paper he had given her with his hotel address and telephone number. Hotel Paloma. The main post office was evidently not far off, according to the map, so she could telephone from there.

She had arrived at the harbour of Mandraki. Two bronze deer on tall columns guarded the entrance and here, it was said, once stood the celebrated Colossus of Rhodes, one of the Seven Wonders of the ancient world.

In the Post Office she telephoned Ray's hotel and was fortunate enough to catch him in.

"I'm sorry I couldn't come to the café. I had to go on working."

"What? Past eight o'clock on a Saturday?" he queried.

"Well, Mr. Brendon – my employer – wanted some documents rather urgently."

"I hope he pays you overtime."

Jacynth laughed. "In this kind of job, you don't really have fixed hours."

"Where are you speaking from now?" Ray asked.

"The main post office near the harbour."

"Oh, in that case, I'll come along and meet you. I take it that your old slave-driver lets you have Sundays off?"

"I've today off," she replied. "I wouldn't guarantee that as a habit."

"Right. I'll be there in about – a quarter of an hour. Walk along the gardens parallel with the harbour. If we miss each other, go to the Café Actaeon. You can't miss that!"

But by the time she had reached the end of the strip of garden, Ray Gurney was hurrying towards her.

"M'm. You look marvellous," he greeted her with enthusiasm. "As a matter of fact, I stayed in the hotel for a while on the offchance that you might ring. Lucky for me!"

At the Café Actaeon there was a choice of tables set under an enormous tree, or those on a raised terrace divided by Moorish arches. Ray ordered coffee and asked about Jacynth's new job.

"Has it come up to your expectations?"

"I don't quite know what I expected, so that's difficult to answer. I assumed that the Villa Kalakos was a small house where I'd be staying and that I'd be going to an office each day to work for Mr. Brendon."

"And it's something different?"

"Yes. It's fairly large and quite imposing in an Italian style, and it's his home."

"I see. So it's more of a residential post. That's bad." Ray shook his head with mock solemnity. "You're always at the man's beck and call. That's what happened last night, I suppose?"

She nodded. "But of course, when you begin any new job, there are difficulties."

"What's he like – this employer? Young? Old?"

"Youngish. A little over thirty, I should think."

"Married?"

Jacynth laughed. "I haven't asked him. I don't see any traces of a wife about the place, but that doesn't rule out the possibility."

"Who else lives in the house? Some sort of staff, I suppose."

"A married couple. Caterina is housekeeper and her husband Nikon seems to attend to the garden. Perhaps he's a sort of handyman as well, looks after Mr. Brendon's car and so on."

Ray frowned. "Sounds a rather rum outfit to me. Not sure I like it."

Jacynth was amused. "Why? What's it to you?"

"Well, I feel I ought to keep an eye on you, as a fellow-countryman."

"But you won't be here for a long visit, will you? When do you return?"

"At the end of next week, but before then I have to go over to Athens. But I shall be back again about Friday, I hope."

"Has your business gone well?" she queried.

"Reasonably. I've been out to several potteries, placed various orders and made other enquiries. Would you like to go to a pottery here?"

She hesitated. "I'd like to, very much, but I don't know if I could arrange to have the time off."

Ray smiled. "Just tell the old slave-driver that you have an important appointment with a fairly presentable young man. If you live in the house, you could offer to make up the time later."

Jacynth had a momentary vision of Mallory Brendon's face if she said just that.

"No, I don't think I'd better promise. After all, I've been here so short a time. I don't want to ask for favours just yet."

"Is he attractive – this boss of yours?"

She considered for a moment, visualising again Mallory's features, the sharp planes of his cheekbones, the dark, sombre eyes, the thick black hair springing from a broad brow, the proud, arrogant tilt of his head.

"By that long pause," interrupted Ray, "I guess that he's a Greek god or something very near. Is he Greek, by the way?"

"He has an English name, but I believe I was told he has Greek ancestry. But he doesn't look like Apollo."

"That's something to be thankful for!" was Ray's slightly

acid comment. "Well, let's plan the day before us. Do you want to see the sights or have you already explored the city?"

Jacynth confessed that this was her first venture out of doors since her arrival.

"My, my! He has caged you up. Come on, then, we'll stroll around the old city."

Ray conducted her through one of the arched gateways in the russet-coloured medieval walls. Jacynth was glad that she was wearing flat-heeled sandals, for the winding roadways were paved with small smooth cobbles and little pebbles. The streets were a fascinating maze of alleys and squares with shops of all kinds selling wines and groceries, rugs and jewellery, leather and lace.

On the right, Ray pointed out the famous Street of the Knights, the hostelries of the Crusaders, each inn with its own distinctive design. Jacynth wanted to walk up there and examine the buildings in more detail, but Ray was already beckoning her towards a shop selling painted pottery.

As they turned a corner, a wider street, paved with large blocks of stone, provided a view up the hill of a mosque with a dazzling white minaret gleaming against the pale blue sky.

"Is it possible to visit the mosque?" she asked.

"I don't know. I've never bothered."

Jacynth decided inwardly that if she really wanted to explore the old city of Rhodes she had better come by herself, then she could dally wherever she pleased. On the other hand she ought to be grateful to Ray for touring her around today so that she had a rough idea of the geography of the place.

Ray was naturally extremely interested in the pottery and ceramic shops and stopped to inspect the stocks of almost every one he saw. He pointed out the various traditional designs in colours and styles as well as what he considered would sell best at home in England.

Eventually, after a prolonged stroll, he and Jacynth emerged by another gate and walked across what looked like an ancient drawbridge of massive stonework. Peering down at the grassy hollow below, Jacynth saw half a dozen cats with twice that number of kittens playing and leaping among the bushes.

"Are they wild?" she asked. "Well, I mean homeless rather than uncivilised. A cat colony, perhaps."

"I suppose so," answered Ray. "Apparently they survive on what they can forage for themselves."

"Oh, no." Her sharp eyes had detected morsels of fish and two small kittens were busily stripping the flesh from part of a fish backbone. "People bring them food sometimes."

Ray took her arm to lead her away. "You're more interested in the cats than in me," he complained. "Let's go and have lunch somewhere."

He took her to a restaurant where an extension had been built out over the waters of the harbour.

"It's like being on a ship," she commented. It was at that moment that the realisation dawned on her. She had come out for the day with only a few drachmas in her purse. True, she had some English money, but she had changed only a small amount into Greek currency before she arrived and had naturally intended to change more at the bank when she needed it. As this was the first opportunity of emerging from the Villa Kalakos, she had not needed money until now.

She glanced surreptitiously at the prices on the menu and was relieved to find that they seemed moderate, for she did not want Ray to spend money on her that he could ill afford.

He ordered *ouzo* as an aperitif. "Have you sampled it yet?"

She shook her head. "No. But last night we had some *retsina* at dinner."

Ray's eyebrows lifted. "We? You dine with the boss, then? I thought you said he was a terrible slave-driver and an old curmudgeon."

That was a bad slip, thought Jacynth. "Oh, that was only once in a blue moon," she said hurriedly. "I usually have my meals alone in the room where I work, but last night we were working so late – he might easily have asked for coffee and sandwiches, but Caterina, his housekeeper, had prepared a meal."

The waiter brought the glasses of *ouzo* and Jacynth took a small sip of the aniseed-flavoured spirit. Ray drank his neat, but she found hers too strong undiluted and was surprised when the added water turned the drink cloudy.

"You'll get used to it in time," Ray assured her, "and prefer it without water."

He ordered a light, simple meal of sea-bream followed by spiced meat-balls called *keftedes*. For some time afterwards he and Jacynth sat talking, while he smoked Greek cigarettes and told her about some of his business encounters with the local pottery manufacturers.

"So I stood firm and beat the salesman down to a lower figure. Oh, he had tears in his eyes as he declared that a few more buyers like me would bankrupt him, but I've heard those tales before."

"Your employers should be proud of you," murmured Jacynth, and was immediately sorry that a slightly sarcastic note had crept into her voice, but Ray apparently noticed nothing, for he continued with even more accounts of his triumphs in bargaining.

At length he suggested that they might walk through some of the new town and look in the shops. Jacynth agreed, but hid her smiles, for "*looking* in the shops" was all she could do with no more than a few drachmas in her possession.

She took out her street map and checked the names of the boulevards as she walked along, for in due course she would need to know the short cuts for her own satisfaction. At one point she and Ray turned a corner and she discovered that now they were close to the Villa Kalakos.

She looked at the top of the windmill as she passed the wall topped by iron railings. "Not everyone can boast of having a windmill in their own garden," she commented.

"Is this where you live?" he asked.

"Yes. Kalakos. But you must have known where it was when you sent me that note yesterday."

Ray laughed. "No. I sent a young boy with it. I knew your address, of course. It was on your luggage, but I'd no idea where the house was. So this is the ogre's castle."

Jacynth was vexed with herself for giving him the information, believing that he already knew. Yet where was the harm? Ray Gurney was only a passing acquaintance, a young Englishman chance-met whose visit to Rhodes would be over in a week. It was unlikely that she would ever see him again.

Facing the shore on the north-west coast were several new hotels, some only in the early stages of erection, others almost finished. She wondered if any were those with which Mallory Brendon was concerned, but no doubt in due course she would find out. It would make her work more interesting if she could see the actual buildings and follow their progress.

"You've gone silent," observed Ray. "Thinking about the great boss? I can see that I'm going to get very jealous of that man."

Jacynth laughed lightly. "No need for that. When I'm out of the house I'm glad to forget about him and his work." To her astonishment, she realised that this was an outright lie. Mallory Brendon occupied her thoughts far more than was necessary, or even prudent. Since she had first started working in offices, she had never cherished any particular fondness for any of her chiefs. Of course, she reflected, they had usually been middle-aged or elderly men with families, sometimes daughters as old as herself. The only man to whom she had been really attracted was David – and he was shortly to marry her cousin Sara. So she must put him firmly out of her thoughts. At this moment she was startled to find that although she had been in Rhodes so short a time, David's image was fading. He seemed very far away.

Jacynth paused now by the promenade rail to watch the sunset tinge the sea to dark mauve and the sky to streaks of pink and gold.

"I'm very annoyed that I'm obliged to leave you here in Rhodes," Ray broke into her reverie. "If I had the time, I'd like to be taking you out every day, show you the sights and all that."

Jacynth smiled gently. "I can't see Mr. Brendon giving me

44

time off every day to go out sightseeing either alone or with an escort."

"It's a darned nuisance that I have to leave for Athens tomorrow. I'll be back on Thursday or Friday and then we could have a whole day together. Ask your boss."

"I can't promise anything," she replied. "It depends on how much work there is to be done."

"Well, let's make the most of the rest of the day we have now. What would you like to do? Go back into the town? We could have dinner somewhere."

"Oh, please, not another meal." Apart from not being hungry, Jacynth was thinking of the financial strain on her companion. "Perhaps a coffee somewhere?"

"Right," he agreed. "Is it too far to walk back or shall we take a taxi?"

"Oh, let's walk."

The coloured lights of the façade of the new Market opposite the harbour, the yachts clustered close to the quays and crowds of people strolling about gave a liveliness to the evening scene that Jacynth thoroughly appreciated.

"So different from our dear old home towns!" she commented. "Everything shut sharp at five and not a soul about anywhere."

Ray took her to one of the cafés along the outside terraces of the market. Almost every table was occupied, waiters dashed about and Jacynth could hear snatches of half a dozen languages among the buzz of conversation.

"This is what I like about Continental places," Ray said, when he found a table. "You can sit and watch the world go by."

She was quite content to do just that for the next hour. Later, Ray ordered what he told her were *mézés*, little snacks served with drinks, and she was happy to pick over a saucer of small fish like sprats.

About ten o'clock, Jacynth suggested going home.

"So early?" queried Ray.

"I haven't a latchkey, and I don't want to wake up Caterina

45

to let me in."

Ray took a taxi this time, as he said it was too far to walk in the dark along the promenade. At the gate of the villa he paid off the driver and accompanied her through the garden.

In the shadow of some tall bushes, Ray took her in his arms and kissed her with more enthusiasm than a good-night kiss seemed to warrant.

Jacynth did not respond, but freed herself as quickly as possible.

"Don't go yet, darling," implored Ray. "Why don't we go into this windmill you showed me? I could kiss you properly then."

"No, Ray," she objected. "It's late already and – "

He pulled her roughly into his arms again and pressed his lips against hers. "I'm longing to come back to Rhodes," he whispered. "Darling, we could have fun – if only – "

This time she wrenched herself out of his grasp and almost ran towards the front door of the villa. "Good-night, Ray!" she called over her shoulder. "Thanks very much for a lovely day!"

She raced up the two wide steps to the porch and cannoned into a solid body leaning against the door. The impact shocked her into a state of nervous apology.

"I'm sorry, Mr. Brendon. I didn't – er – see you there."

"I'm well aware of that," Mallory Brendon replied calmly. "I didn't think you'd dive-bomb at me if you knew I was there."

She swallowed some large obstruction in her throat and groped for words. When none came – or at least none that made sense – she took refuge in a stammered "Good-night, Mr. Brendon."

"I'm glad you had a good day," he murmured, "and evidently good company. It seems that you're on very friendly terms with him. Someone you met here?"

She was aware that in her light-coloured clothes she must have been plainly visible to Mallory when Ray had grasped her in his arms.

"The young man I met at Athens airport and who accompanied me to Rhodes," she said coldly. It was no business of her employer to catechise her about acquaintances with whom she spent her, so far, very limited free time.

"Oh, you've been able to communicate with him, then?"

"He was able to communicate with me," she retorted. "He felt that he had a certain responsibility towards me."

"How did he know your address unless you gave it to him?"

"I didn't give it. The name of the villa was on my luggage labels."

"I see." Mallory took a puff at his cigar. "Then in future I'd be obliged if you'd be more discreet. I don't want dozens of young men calling on you here – and distracting you."

Anger welled up in Jacynth. "You can rest assured, Mr. Brendon, that there's no need for alarm on your part. I'm not likely to attract these dozens of young men you mention. As for Ray – Mr. Gurney, he's here on business for only a short visit. He returns tomorrow."

In the darkness Mallory gave a subdued chuckle. "I don't know whether to give you my condolences on that account or congratulate you on making the most of your time."

In an impulsive movement her hand lifted sharply, but she arrested it before it could land on his face in a stinging slap. "Perhaps you would allow me to pass," she said furiously. He was blocking the door.

"Certainly." He moved aside, but in her haste to get away from this mocking creature, Jacynth brushed his arm and was surprised at the confusing and weakening effect the contact had on her.

She almost ran across the dimly-lit hall towards the stairs.

"Eight o'clock start tomorrow morning!" he called, and she turned sharply on the stair. "I like to begin early. Also, when the weather becomes hotter in the summer, we have siesta timetables."

He was standing at the foot of the stairs, an orange lantern glinting on his dark hair and upturned face.

"I'll be ready!" she called back, and fled up to her room. She flopped on the bed, shaken by seething anger but also by the way hot colour flooded into her cheeks and her heart leapt about when she unavoidably barged into him.

It had been bad enough to collide with him that first time in the porch. That unexpected encounter had knocked her off balance, both physically and emotionally. The second time was worse and could have been avoided if she had observed rather more dignity in escaping indoors. Yet, she muttered angrily aloud, what gave him the right to spy on her, lurking about hidden in doorways?

She should have asked him that question before rushing away so ignominiously. She vowed that next time she would demand an answer. At the same time she remembered with a sigh that she was here in Rhodes working for Mr. Brendon on only an exceedingly temporary basis. At any moment he could pack her off to England, not only on the grounds of incompetence, but probably because he would maintain that temperamentally she was unfitted to continue in the job.

Jacynth sniffed away a tear or two of self-pity and wondered what further humiliations might be in store.

CHAPTER THREE

WHEN Jacynth went down to her office next morning at ten minutes to eight, she found Mallory Brendon already there. He was scribbling notes and corrections on some of the immaculately-typed foolscap sheets she had worked on during Saturday.

"These will have to be done again," he murmured without looking up or even giving her a good-morning.

"*Kalimera*," she said pointedly.

He looked up sharply as she sat in front of her typewriter. "*Kalimera*," he replied. "Is that one of your half-dozen words of Greek?"

His voice was as taunting as ever, but this morning there was the hint of a smile around his mouth and his dark eyes held a sparkle of amusement, so perhaps he was inclined to be more amiable than last evening.

"I'm trying to learn a few expressions so that I can find my way about," she answered evenly.

He smiled at her and his eyes lost that amused expression, if it had ever been there. "Are you sure that you'll be here long enough to use your Greek?"

She flushed. He had scored another point. So he was still holding over her the threat of dismissing her.

"Even on a fortnight's holiday in a foreign country, I still think it courteous to try to learn a few words," she said without looking at him.

He gave a subdued exclamation of laughter. "Neatly rebuked! I see I must be more careful in future how I frame my questions."

She took the amended sheets of foolscap that he now handed to her.

"Those will keep you busy for part of the day," he told her,

49

"but before you tackle those I want you to come to my study now. I have some information I've been waiting for and I can now dictate the rest of that contract we had to leave the other day."

She followed him to the large study he used in another part of the house and for the next hour concentrated on taking down the complicated conditions of a new contract for financing an hotel along the coast.

"You'd better make a rough draft of that," he instructed. "There may be alterations."

"Very well. Shall I do this first?"

"Yes. If you could knock it out by about eleven o'clock, I'd be glad."

She nodded.

"By the way, at last the London office have sent me the confirming letter about substituting a Miss Jacynth Rowan for Diana Osborn. They claim that they sent a telegram, but evidently that went astray somewhere."

"I'm sorry you didn't get the girl you expected," she murmured.

"I have yet to discover whether that will turn out an advantage or otherwise," he said drily. "Did you know Diana?"

"Oh, yes. She was in a different department, but we used to meet sometimes."

"Very different from you." Under his scrutiny she felt the fiery colour rising fast in her cheeks.

"I could never compete with her. She's very attractive and – sophisticated, too."

"Probably," he agreed. "Yes, you're quite a contrasting type. Fair hair, blue eyes – the English look."

The way he said it made it sound as though she were very insipid-looking. She remembered Diana with her masses of dark hair round her shoulders, mischievous brown eyes and an eminently kissable mouth that probably had a long record of service.

"And did you go shopping yesterday?" was his next query when she did not answer what she thought an unanswerable comment. "Diana was everlasting pottering around the shops."

"Actually, no. I found I had very few drachmas and had omitted to take sterling with me to cash."

"Then it was fortunate that your boy-friend took you out for the day and, I presume, gave you something to eat?"

"Yes," she admitted. "I shan't be so careless next time."

He chuckled. "Does that mean that you have these quality ideas? Share and share alike? He pays one time and you pay the other?"

She laughed. "Not exactly. In any case, Ray is not my boy-friend. I haven't known him long."

"Long enough for a prolonged good-night embrace last night."

A spark of mischief entered her head. "If I'd known you were standing there, I might have encouraged him to spin it out longer."

"Would you indeed?" His dark brows converged in a frown. "You'd better start on that draft," he said abruptly. The amiable mood was over. Jacynth was dismissed.

As she typed the complicated phrases and clauses, part of her mind was occupied by thoughts of her employer. Evidently he could make sarcastic remarks no matter whether they wounded or not, but she must not exchange the same currency with him.

Bother the man! Thinking about him caused her to make mistakes. A blessing this document was only a first draft. However, she managed to finish it in reasonable shape by the time he came in demanding it.

She had just poured herself a cup of coffee from the pot Caterina had brought and absent-mindedly Mallory helped himself to the solitary cup.

"Right!" he said briskly as he picked up the draft, "I'll take this with me to the conference. You've plenty to get on with for the rest of the day."

Indeed she had! Some of the documents were twenty pages thick.

At the door he paused and looked back at her. "And the siesta season hasn't started yet!" was his final warning as he went out.

Jacynth let out a long gasping sigh of relief. Too much of his presence was more than she could stand, yet the room seemed empty and devoid of vitality without his masculine dynamism.

She poured out another cup of coffee from the pot and experienced a thrill of pleasure at the idea of sharing the same cup, even if a trifle unhygienic.

What absurdity! Really, she must shake herself out of this ludicrous day-dreaming and apply herself to Mr. Brendon's tasks or she would find herself day-dreaming on the way home to England.

After lunch she walked about the grounds of the villa, where Nikon was tidying the rock garden behind the swimming pool, still empty and forlorn with dust and dead leaves.

"When do you fill the pool with water?" she asked him in half Greek, half English.

"In April," he told her. That was easy, for the names of the months were fairly similar to those in English.

She left him to his task and wandered among the shrubs, many of them already in blossom, oleander and paeonies, with other kinds which she had never seen before. Pines and cypresses were sited where they would afford shade in the summer months and in one corner of the garden was a small summerhouse, with a conical roof of intertwined branches. On one of the wooden uprights of the door were initials carved deeply. "KTZ" and underneath "OEP". She wondered who had been the original inhabitants of the villa, whether it was the family home of Mallory Brendon or if, as she considered more likely, he merely rented it as a residence also serving as a business apartment.

When she returned indoors, it occurred to her that so far she had not even seen the other rooms in the villa apart from Mr. Brendon's study and the small crowded room on the other side of the hall where she had waited on the day of her arrival.

She asked Caterina if she might look in the downstairs rooms, since at this moment there was little chance of disturbing her employer. He would not be back until the evening, so the housekeeper confirmed.

Caterina accompanied Jacynth and identified each room in turn, but that was hardly necessary, for the dining room with an oval walnut table and chairs with tapestry seats and richly carved backs proclaimed its use. The drawing room – Jacynth thought it was too large and spacious to be called a sitting-room – had pale turquoise walls with elaborate cornices and a handsome ceiling. There were comfortable-looking arm-chairs upholstered in modern fabrics and groups of other chairs arranged around small tables. At the far end near the wide french windows was a full-size grand piano and Jacynth wondered if Mallory played. Gilt-framed mirrors reflected each other on opposite sides of the room and large porcelain vases and urns stood on the white marble mantelpiece and on tables.

The room appeared to be well kept, but Jacynth thought rarely used and Caterina confirmed this. Mr. Brendon did not come in it unless he entertained visitors.

Jacynth giggled. She could scarcely imagine Mallory Brendon acting as host to a gathering of assorted people. Presiding at a board table was more in his line.

On the opposite side of the house there were two rooms between Jacynth's office and Mallory's study. One was a library with well-filled shelves and leather armchairs. A man's room, obviously, and perhaps it was here that Mallory usually entertained his cronies. The other room was apparently locked and Caterina said she had no key.

"Bluebeard's chamber," said Jacynth, but the other woman did not understand the allusion, repeating that it was never used.

Jacynth was intrigued, but did not press the point. So Mallory kept a room locked. To hide some secret in his past?

Or merely to practise a hobby?

The rest of the day was occupied in hard work and Jacynth decided to continue until half-past seven to make up for the time she had dawdled away at lunch-time.

She heard Mallory's car just as she came out of her office and dodged back again inside. She did not want him to believe that she was waiting to welcome him on the mat in his own home.

She picked up several files as though she were tidying them when he came striding in and flopped in the nearest chair.

"God! I've had a day!" he muttered.

"Can I get you anything? A drink?"

He waved his hand impatiently. "Don't start trying to mother me. You can safely leave that to Caterina."

However tired he might be or disappointed over some business worry, his tongue had lost nothing of its sharp edge.

Jacynth hesitated, uncertain whether to leave or stay. Over his shoulder he said, "Tell Caterina to bring me a brandy."

She hastened out to the kitchen, only too relieved to have some definite message, but apprehensive in case she muddled his order and the housekeeper brought him a glass of milk. She guessed that the word "cognac" might sound the same in Greek and watched while the woman poured a large glass of brandy and added the bottle, with a bottle of mineral water to the tray.

She motioned to Jacynth to take the tray, but the girl shook her head and followed Caterina at a discreet distance. Jacynth did not want to be accused twice in a few minutes of trying to "mother" her employer!

When she arrived in the office, Mallory was speaking in Greek to the housekeeper. Jacynth waited until the woman left to return to the kitchen and while Mallory took a large gulp of his brandy.

"Do you want me to – ?" she began tentatively.

"No," he interrupted. "Everything can wait until the morning." After a slight pause he asked, "Have you finished all the work I gave you?"

54

She half smiled. "Not all of it. I kept to the order that you'd indicated, but there are still several schedules to do." In her turn she paused, then added, "You didn't really expect me to complete the lot, did you?"

He gazed at her across the table and again that disturbing current flowed through her veins, undermining the cool, businesslike but friendly attitude she was trying to create.

"I don't really know your capabilities, Miss Rowan," he said with that elusive smile playing around his mouth.

"Well, I haven't slacked all day – just because you weren't standing at my elbow!" She was aghast at her loss of temper. "I'm sorry, Mr. Brendon. I shouldn't have said that."

"If you thought that way, why shouldn't you say so? No need to bottle it up. I prefer people to be honest."

She doubted very much whether he preferred all his business associates to be honest and frank about their own plans. She was well aware that secrecy, camouflage and sometimes false information innocently disclosed were all apparently desirable in the kind of financial deals in which he was involved.

He took another deep draught of brandy and passed a hand across his forehead, ruffling his thick dark hair in the process.

"Go away and leave me now," he muttered. "Have your dinner and meet your boy-friend, if that's what you intended."

There was no point in reminding him that Ray had left for Athens and she went quietly out of the room.

In her room while she changed her dress, applied fresh make-up and brushed her pale corn-coloured hair, she reflected that Mallory was occasionally vulnerable. The mask of the hundred per cent business man fell, if only for a short time, and behind it was a man, subject to the frets and ills of day-to-day encounters. In a way she was glad, for even a moment's weakness made him seem more human.

She waited another quarter of an hour before going down in case he remained in her office. Then the idea struck her that perhaps he was intending to dine with her and discuss the business of the day – that is, as much as he ever disclosed to her. He needed to unwind and she would be his undemanding companion.

But a first glance into the office told her that no tête-à-tête dinner was arranged. One place was laid as usual and Mallory's tray with bottles and glass had been removed. No doubt he was dining alone in solitary state in the handsome room she had seen for the first time this afternoon.

Jacynth experienced a keen sense of disappointment, even though he had certainly given her no encouragement to believe that he would still be there. Apart from a faint aroma of cigar smoke, the room seemed empty and lifeless without his vital masculine presence.

Caterina had evidently been waiting to serve the meal and now she brought in the first course, a shrimp and tomato salad with a very piquant sauce. Jacynth was surprised when this was followed by a large turkey, studded with chestnuts and raisins and Caterina proceeded to carve off several succulent slices. The dish of vegetables as accompaniment – artichokes and aubergines, with beans of a shape unknown to Jacynth, contained enough to serve three or four people and she had to refuse too large a helping of each. Pastry with a creamy custard filling and preserved plums on top and finally a crumbly yellow cheese called *kaseri*.

When Caterina came to clear away and serve coffee, Jacynth complimented her on such a superb meal and the woman's eyes glowed with pleasure. She murmured a few words which Jacynth understood to mean roughly that it was better for food to be eaten than to cook for nothing.

"Mr. Brendon has already eaten?" she queried.

"No. Only an omelette and a glass of wine."

Now she understood Caterina's rather dour remark about cooking for nothing. It seemed that Jacynth herself had been treated to first cut of all the courses.

A voice in the hall calling "Caterina!" sent the housekeeper hurrying out. Jacynth could hear Mallory speaking in rapid Greek to the woman and through the half open door she could see him, in evening dress now and obviously going out somewhere important. He spoke incisively and his weariness seemed to have vanished. In a few moments the front door slammed and soon there was the sound of his car as he drove off.

Caterina returned to the room where Jacynth sat drinking her coffee. She collected the remaining dishes on to a tray and smiled as though enjoying a joke.

"Mr. Brendon has gone out, then?" Jacynth remarked, confirming the obvious.

Caterina muttered that it was possible he had gone to see his Greek girl. She hurried out of the room before Jacynth could ask any further questions.

His Greek girl? Jacynth felt a hollowness that disturbed and annoyed her. Surely it was only natural that Mallory should have numerous friends and acquaintances on the island and that among them would be some beautiful girls. Not only Greek, either, but any nationality that might come within the aura of that "irresistible" personality that Diana Osborn had mentioned.

But was there one special one? Jacynth realised that she did not even know if Mallory were married. Certainly no Mrs. Mallory Brendon lived in the Villa Kalakos at the present time, but she might be in some other part of the world. He might be a widower, divorced, merely separated. It was difficult to imagine that with his male magnetism he had so far eluded matrimony altogether.

Jacynth shook herself as though to chase away these absurd thoughts. What did it matter to her if he had gone out tonight to meet half a dozen Greek or French or Italian girls? But the answer ricocheted back to her at once. Let him have his fun with half a dozen, but if there were only one special girl-friend, Jacynth would hope that whoever it was would be worthy of Mallory.

Now she laughed at herself for these righteous ideas. Why trouble herself about her employer's love-life when she would be working for him for only the next three or four months? Even less if he sacked her earlier.

She went to bed fairly early and read for more than an hour. Once or twice she thought she heard the sound of a car returning, but her bedroom was nearer the back of the villa and it was unlikely she could distinguish one distant noise from another.

She shut the book with a bang and switched out her reading lamp, unwilling to admit to herself that her ears were on the alert for Mallory's homecoming. It was more important, she told herself, to get a good night's sleep and be fit for the morning and its problems and difficulties.

For the next two days the work seemed to go smoothly, although she saw little of Mallory, for he was either out of the house or occupied in his study with instructions not to be disturbed. There were minor disturbances, one when she failed to find the correct batch of photographs of "Project N" to attach to a schedule. The hotels were labelled with letters of the alphabet, for usually the actual names were not chosen until the buildings were completed.

"I gave you the right prints yesterday," Mallory complained. "Have you lost them?"

Jacynth returned to her office and searched for the large envelope labelled "Project N". Eventually she found the missing photographs in the wrong envelope. She suspected that the fault lay with Mallory, but it would be useless to tell him so. No doubt he regarded himself as infallible.

Jacynth realised that on such incidents depended the future of her job here, and even if she considered she was blameless, she must learn not to complain.

So she was both surprised and delighted when later in the week he said suddenly, "I want you to come with me tomorrow evening to the Grand Summer Palace – that's the luxury hotel a little way out of the town. Be ready about eight o'clock."

"Very well." She was about to ask him if she should have her dinner first or whether something would be provided at the hotel, but he forestalled her.

"I know you have an excellent appetite and I don't want you

feeling faint, so ask Caterina for a snack at some convenient time."

"Anyone would think I thought of nothing but food," she retorted mildly.

"And don't you? Caterina tells me you can put away quite sizeable meals. She likes that and says you're worth cooking for." He glanced up at her, his dark eyes glittering with amusement. "More than I am, I'm afraid. She grumbles when I spoil her dishes by my irregular hours."

"Perhaps I ought to watch my diet," she suggested. "I might put on too much weight with such good Greek food."

He surveyed her, his eyes travelling up and down her figure as she stood near his desk. Today she was wearing a turquoise blue jersey dress, clipped in at the waist with an antique gold belt and, under his scrutiny, she wished she had been wearing a shapeless sack that did not reveal the soft curve of her breasts.

She knew the hot colour was flooding up into her cheeks, and was irritated that she could not control it when Mallory's eyes held hers with a strange, compelling quality.

"I doubt if you need worry about weight-watching yet," he said at last, then added abruptly, "All right, that's all."

She hurried out of his study as though pursued by demons. In the privacy of her office, she sagged on to a chair. What on earth was the matter with her? It was plainly idiotic and absurd to find herself trembling and slightly breathless now as if she had been running. Oh, she had plenty of experience of working for various chiefs in her business life and knew the value of being on the same wavelength. But this strange turbulence that assailed her so often in Mallory's presence was beyond all reasoning. She was acting like a silly schoolgirl of fifteen or so.

Yet she was flattered that he had asked her to accompany him to this reception, conference or whatever it was at the Grand Summer Palace. In her mind she surveyed her not very extensive wardrobe, but reminded herself that she was not supposed to dress up as though she were being taken out dancing.

Dancing? She closed her eyes and tried to imagine the heady pleasure of being held in Mallory's arms and circling a ballroom floor, but thrust that vision away. She was at it again, conjuring up the most ridiculously impossible fancies.

Jacynth was finishing off her work next afternoon when Caterina came in to tell her she was wanted on the telephone. Mallory was out somewhere, so she naturally assumed he would be the caller, perhaps to give her some instructions.

In his study she answered, "Yes, Mr. Brendon?"

A different voice replied, "But it isn't your marvellous Mr. Brendon. It's me – Ray. Ray Gurney. Remember?"

"Oh – er – yes. What is it?"

"I've just arrived back from Athens and I have the most marvellous news. Can you come out with me tonight?"

"No, I'm afraid I can't," she said quickly.

"Well, why not? You don't have to slave all hours still for the man, do you?"

"It isn't that. I have to go with him to a – a business meeting."

"Oh? Is that what he calls it?" drawled Ray.

"That's what it is," answered Jacynth sharply. But she was not disposed to tell Ray the place of the meeting. It was essential to be discreet if she were to retain Mallory's trust and confidence by not discussing his business affairs with outsiders.

"What time will you be through?" queried Ray.

"I can't possibly know that."

"And what is it that you can't possibly know?" Mallory had entered the room.

She looked up guiltily, although there was no need. He had not forbidden her to have incoming calls.

"May I know who the caller is – unless it's a personal one of yours?"

"It's Ray – Mr. Gurney."

The expression of sardonic satisfaction on Mallory's face almost made her jam down the receiver, but at the other end of the line Ray was impatiently muttering, "What's up? Is

60

someone else there? Hallo!"

"Oh, your boy-friend! Then carry on, by all means. Did he want you to go out with him?"

Jacynth was furious with herself for being trapped into the admission, with Ray for telephoning at this precise moment and, unreasonably, with Mallory for his untimely appearance.

"It doesn't matter," she said abruptly. Then, to Ray, "I'm sorry, Ray, but I'll have to go now. I can't come anyway."

As she was about to cut off, Mallory prevented her by holding her wrist. "Tell him you'll see him tomorrow," he said. "You can have the afternoon and evening off, if you want to."

In almost a daze, Jacynth nodded. The touch of Mallory's fingers on her wrist had been quite unnerving, sending shivers of excitement through her body.

Into the phone she said, "I could manage tomorrow, if that would suit you."

"O.K., that'll be fine," answered Ray. "Although I can see that I have to take second place to your illustrious boss. Right, then. Seven o'clock at the Actaeon?"

"Yes. Seven o'clock." Jacynth was only too eager to put down the receiver.

To Mallory she said, "I'm sorry about that. I don't encourage telephone calls in business hours."

"No need to apologise," Mallory said, almost airily. "I wouldn't wish to deprive you of simple pleasures, especially as you haven't had the chance of making many friends here in Rhodes."

Now that he had sat down in his usual chair facing his desk, it occurred to her that she was dangerously close to him, so near that if he had been the flirtatious kind of employer, he could have pulled her down on to his lap with a single movement.

She moved a yard away from him to the corner of his desk. Not that her proximity mattered to him. But it was important to her and she drove out of her mind those embarrassing thoughts.

"Thank you, Mr. Brendon, for tomorrow evening," she

said quietly. "Will that be all now?"

"Er – yes," he muttered, already busy with a sheaf of papers he had taken from his briefcase. As she reached the door, he looked up. "Oh, there's just one thing. I take it you've learned to be careful about talking business matters with friends."

"Oh, yes," Jacynth answered emphatically. "I've had good training in that respect at the London office."

He nodded once or twice. "Then you understand how important it is that no cats are let out of bags before the right moment."

"Naturally." Then she added, "I didn't tell Ray, of course, where we were going tonight. I just said it was a business meeting."

His dark eyes seemed to be measuring her truthfulness. "All right." As she turned to go, he added, "If you want to use the phone, you're at liberty to do so, provided I'm not on the line myself."

At last he let her go as she murmured, "Thank you."

Back in her office she gazed unseeingly at her covered typewriter. Why must she always become so excited and disturbed whenever she encountered Mallory Brendon? She could find no sane answer to this silly question, except to resolve that in future she would be the cool girl who could work for a devastatingly attractive employer without being affected in the least. Concentration on the work itself, not on the man connected with it.

After a quick snack that Caterina provided, Jacynth went to her room and took a brisk shower in the adjoining bathroom. What sort of dress to wear for an eight o'clock rendezvous at the Grand Summer Palace? That question was soon settled, for her choice lay between a long skirt of patterned voile worn with a filmy white blouse or a knee-length dress of white cotton printed with green ferns.

She settled for the short dress. If she tried to look too conscious of being taken out for the evening by her boss, he would no doubt have some sharp comments to make.

Now she twisted her fair hair into a bun and tied it with a

green ribbon. Careful make-up, eye-shadow not too pronounced and mascara lightly applied, she viewed herself in the long mirror. A perfume spray of subtle delicacy which she had brought with her from London and she was ready.

When Mallory came into her office downstairs where she had elected to wait for him, she thought he gave her a glance of approval, but he said nothing except, "If you're ready, we'll go."

She picked up her handbag and a lacy white shawl and followed him to the car, waiting until he indicated that she was to sit next to him in the passenger seat.

"Got your notebook and pen?" he enquired.

"Of course," she answered levelly.

He laughed softly. "Not to be caught out this time? I doubt whether you'll need them."

On the short drive to the hotel, Jacynth tried to calm herself. It was not merely the thrill of being taken out for the first time by Mallory for an evening jaunt, even if it were only on business. What tormented her was his nearness, the sheer masculine aura that enveloped her like a cloud, both exhilarating and dismaying at the same time.

Jacynth had only a glimpse of the blaze of lights streaming from the hotel when she scrambled out quickly from her side of the car and waited while Mallory locked it. He escorted her across a reception hall and into a lift, finally along a corridor and into a large room filled with people standing or sitting about, white-jacketed waiters moving deftly with trays of drinks. More than half the assembly appeared to be women, so obviously this was not exactly a business conference.

Mallory was at her elbow now, introducing her to several young women, all exquisitely dressed. Jacynth acknowledged shyly, aware that she was already dismissed in their minds as a nonentity.

"And, Hermione, this is my secretary, Miss Rowan. Miss Perandopoulos."

Jacynth found herself facing one of the most beautiful girls she had ever seen. Slightly taller than herself, but not reaching Mallory's height, Hermione Perandopoulos seemed to have every possible lovely feminine feature rolled into one. Gleaming hair, blue-black as a raven's wing, luminous hazel eyes, a creamy skin and the softest rose-petal mouth.

She smiled acknowledgment at Jacynth, then turned towards Mallory. "Your new secretary is quite different from your usual type. What happened to that other girl who was here a few months ago – the dark one with mischief in her eyes?"

"Ah," sighed Mallory in mock grief, "I'm afraid she's now married."

Hermione's arched eyebrows rose in surprise. "Obviously she must have found you wanting in charm – or perhaps other assets. It could hardly be wealth, unless her husband is a multi-millionaire."

"I've no idea who her husband is," replied Mallory, "so I can't tell you what he possesses that I lack."

Hermione laughed. "It's clear that you don't possess the girl!" She gave an appraising glance at Jacynth, who interpreted the look as speculative. This beautiful Greek girl, evidently on extremely friendly terms with Mallory, was sizing up his new secretary.

Jacynth maintained what she hoped was an amiable expression under this deceptively casual scrutiny. If Hermione imagined that she had a new rival, Jacynth could have speedily reassured her. Mallory was hardly likely to waste his attentions on his typist when Hermione Perandopoulos was available.

Mallory at this moment stopped a passing waiter and handed drinks to Hermione and Jacynth. "Let's sit down somewhere, shall we?" he suggested. But someone else came to claim Hermione and bore her away on his arm to a knot of people on the far side of the room.

Mallory chose two chairs placed round a vacant table. Then he said in a quiet, intense voice, "Have you a good memory, Miss Rowan?"

"I think so. I hope so," she amended.

64

"We shall be joined some time during the evening by that plump man talking to three or four other people. I don't want you to write down anything, but listen and try to remember the gist of the conversation. If there's an opportunity and you're comparatively alone, write down brief notes. You understand?"

"Perfectly."

"He's coming across here now, right on cue," murmured Mallory with a smile. A moment later he greeted the other man, "Hallo, Carlyon," and the two men shook hands. Mallory introduced Jacynth and the newcomer sat down on the opposite side of Mallory. For a few minutes the conversation was no more than trivial remarks about the present party and some of the people present. Then Mr. Carlyon, who had an American accent, leaned nearer to Mallory and asked, "Has he been given the go-ahead?"

"Not yet," was Mallory's answer.

"Then we still have time," said the other.

Jacynth shifted her position slightly so that she could hear without appearing to listen too keenly. So far, this was easy enough, but soon the exchange between the two men became more involved. At times, she failed to hear more than half a sentence, and none of what was said made sense. She cast a beseeching look at Mallory when she caught his eye, but he swerved his attention immediately back to his companion.

Then two more men joined the trio and Jacynth inwardly despaired. She had experience of taking down verbatim meetings, but to keep it all in her head was an impossible task. The other men, however, talked of yacht-racing and drew Mallory and Mr. Carlyon into that topic. With relief, Jacynth caught the slight shake of the head that Mallory gave her.

"Come along, we must circulate," exclaimed Mr. Carlyon, "or the ladies will have our blood."

Mallory laughed a trifle scornfully. "I doubt if any of them have even noticed our temporary absence."

"Very self-effacing of you, Brendon," chimed in one of the others. "When you're at a reception or any other do and ladies are present, you're usually surrounded by a cluster of beauties. No one else gets a look in."

The men laughed at this sally and Mallory smiled in a good-humoured way. He put a hand on Jacynth's elbow to guide her towards the long buffet tables at the side of the room, ignoring the waiters who hovered with trays of delicacies.

At his touch fire ran up her arm and she scarcely heard what he was saying. "Pick out a few odds and ends for yourself. And don't worry if you can't remember all that was said. We'll sort it out later."

Mechanically she helped herself to canapés and petits fours, lobster patties and Turkish delight and little chocolate mounds, not even thinking of the proper order of the food. By the time she had turned away from the tables, Mallory had vanished.

Perhaps that was just as well, she reflected. She needed time to recover from his quicksilver moods, scolding one moment, reassuring her the next. Besides, she was irritated with her own behaviour, her pulses throbbing wildly just because he had absentmindedly shepherded her across a room as he might have offered to see an old lady across a busy street.

Jacynth moved away and sought a not too crowded corner of the room. Almost immediately Mr. Carlyon, Mallory's American business friend, approached her, found her a chair, then one for himself.

"Do you like working for Brendon?" he asked.

"Very much," she answered quickly, even though her reply was half a lie, for there were times when she was anything but relaxed.

"He's a brilliant man at his job," continued Mr. Carlyon. "Any company who can count on his services is very lucky."

A warning bell sounded in Jacynth's mind. With Mallory absent, was his associate about to pump her for information? If so, he would be disappointed, for she had been working for Mallory for too short a period to be able to give coherent information.

She bit into a lobster patty and waited.

"Of course," continued her companion, "he's endowed with most of the desirable qualities, handsome looks, strong physique, but his intellect puts him on a far higher plane than anything else. He has the most uncanny knack – call it instinct, I suppose – of knowing what goes on in other people's minds. He's already argued out his case long before the other chap has even got around to formulating what he wants."

Jacynth nodded intelligently as she munched a small chocolate mound. "Have you known him long?" she asked politely.

"A year or two. Most of my business is in the States and I'm not over in Europe very often, but when we meet, Brendon and I, it's always a pleasure, even if we happen to be rivals on some project or other. You know that whatever the outcome, he can be relied upon to be fair and honest, and that's a pretty difficult proposition in business matters these days."

"Yes, I'm sure it is," Jacynth murmured, realising that whatever she said was only by way of punctuation in Mr. Carlyon's monologue.

"I'm surprised that he hasn't married before now," he went on.

Jacynth gave him her attention, for this was a topic shrouded in ignorance so far. Naturally, she told herself, she was curious to know something of her employer's matrimonial status.

"Perhaps he hasn't found the right girl," she hazarded.

"And perhaps, at last, he has – although he's known her some time. The Perandopoulos heiress is quite a prize. You know that her father is the shipping magnate, owns tankers, liners, docks and the rest."

"I've heard the name."

"Might be quite a good match," Mr. Carlyon warmed to his matchmaking subject. "She's half Greek, half Italian, and he had an English father but a Greek mother. So the combination could be quite interesting."

Jacynth had gone cold, although there was no reason why

she should merely because Mallory's name was being linked with that of Hermione Perandopoulos.

"Brendon would make an excellent son-in-law for the father's enormous interests. He'd rule that empire very efficiently."

"Of course." Her thoughts wandered away. Certainly the business and commercial aspect of such a marriage would no doubt be impeccable, but was that all? Did Mallory demand nothing else but a beautiful hostess at the head of his table and for himself the power of holding the reins of a successful organisation? No love? Not on either side?

Mr. Carlyon's voice interrupted her musings. "Here they come!"

Jacynth looked up to see Mallory approaching with Hermione at his side, her bare arm linked through his, the white skin contrasting with the black sleeve of his dinner jacket.

Almost immediately the pair were surrounded by other people, both men and women, as though they were magnetically drawn to perhaps the most handsome and virile man in the room and certainly the most exquisite girl.

Hermione moved away, circled by her admirers, and Mallory remained standing and watching her progress.

"So Carlyon was talking to you?" he said now to Jacynth. "He's a terrible old gossip."

A glance around her told her that Mr. Carlyon had moved away.

"I expect he's been telling you all the scandal of the island," continued Mallory.

Jacynth laughed lightly. "Some of it, but I didn't really take a lot of notice."

"Just as well. He's a good chap, but like so many Americans, incurably romantic, endlessly arranging imaginary marriages between the most unlikely people. You'd think he was a one-man marriage bureau."

Jacynth's spirits lifted. So it was unnecessary to take the idea of an engagement between Mallory and Hermione too seriously. The item was just one of a number invented by an "incurably romantic" American.

The reception went on endlessly, it seemed to her, yet at no time did she want it to end too soon. Mallory circulated among his friends and acquaintances and sometimes left her to chat with people in small groups. On one of these occasions, three quite lovely girls gathered around Jacynth, asking eager questions in Greek. Only one of them spoke English and at one point, she cut in sharply, "The English girl will be trained not to reply to foolish questions."

Jacynth would dearly have liked to comprehend those foolish questions, but the same girl whispered, "Miss Perandopoulos is looking this way and her glances towards you are not kind."

With a smile and a friendly wave of the hand, the girl crossed the room towards the buffet.

In a way, Jacynth was not too displeased when Mallory decided to go home. She was still trying to retain the gist of that whispered, disjointed conversation between Mallory and Mr. Carlyon. One more glass of wine and she'd be too dizzy to remember anything.

In the car going home, Mallory said, "Just tell me briefly the points you heard. That talk with Carlyon, I mean."

Jacynth flushed red in the darkness. "I had no chance of escaping anywhere and jotting anything down, but this is what I gathered." She told him her version of what had been said. "It doesn't seem to make sense," she admitted. "I'm sorry."

To her astonishment he laughed and impulsively, apparently, put out his right hand and patted her left as it lay in her lap. "You did well, Jacynth. Very well. You know some of the details of my work and the projects I'm engaged on, yet you couldn't string the phrases together to mean anything. So Carlyon and I are pretty sure that if anyone else overheard us, they wouldn't be able to do any better."

His words poured over her without her taking them in. His hand had only momentarily touched hers, yet she was still tingling from that contact. Only later, when she was alighting from the car, did she remember that for the first time he had called her by her Christian name.

"Thank you for taking me," she said, when he was locking and bolting the front door. "But I thought it was a business conference only, so I'm afraid I wasn't dressed properly for the occasion."

"On the contrary, you looked quite charming." Was it mock gallantry that she detected in his voice?

She was standing at the foot of the staircase under a large lantern that shed only a dim light and she was unaware that her corn-coloured hair was burnished to a glow or that the shadows and highlights on her face made her look vulnerable.

Mallory's face was entirely in shadow, yet she knew that he was regarding her with that fierce scrutiny that played havoc with her emotions.

"At least I could have put on a long skirt," she managed to say at last. "I was the only girl there in a short dress."

His head moved and she knew his glance had switched down towards her feet.

"But you have very pretty legs."

This was too much for Jacynth, who murmured a hasty "Good-night" and fled up the stairs as fast as those "pretty legs" could carry her.

In her room she flung off the lacy shawl she had draped over her shoulders and sat down in front of the dressing table, pulling out the hairpins from her coiled hair, and letting it flow loose. She rested her elbows on the table and dropped her head into her hands. Oh, why must he tease her with these insincere remarks? She knew perfectly well now why he had taken her to this so-called conference. That idiotic conversation between him and the man Carlyon had been only a trivial blind. Mallory's real purpose was to demonstrate to her that he was very much sought after by any number of girls and women, even middle-aged ones who lured him on to settees and engaged him in playful teasing.

Most of all, he had been at pains to show her the girl who was probably destined to be the future Mrs. Mallory Brendon, the lovely Hermione. It looked to Jacynth that Hermione would be very willing indeed to occupy that position.

CHAPTER FOUR

JACYNTH wondered as she worked during the following morning whether Mallory would remember his promise to let her have the afternoon and evening off. If any urgent matter came up, her own private arrangements would be speedily cancelled, she was quite sure.

About midday, however, he came into her office and glanced through the work she had completed. He gave several grunts, but whether of satisfaction or displeasure she could not be entirely sure.

"What time are you meeting your boy-friend? Was it seven?" he asked abruptly.

"Yes, that's right."

"In that case you don't need to dally your time in Rhodes. I can fill the intervening hours with more important matters."

She stared at him with a mutinous expression in her blue eyes. "But, Mr. Brendon, you said last night – "

"Oh, last night!" He waved away any such previous obligations. "I didn't know then that I might have to make demands on your time."

She rose and stood in front of her table. "Mr. Brendon," she began coolly, "I'm willing to work twelve hours a day, seven days a week – if that's what you want. But when I'm granted a few hours of free time, I expect it to be honoured. Otherwise, it's quite useless for me to make any plans at all."

He grinned at her in the most disarming way. "You're testy hits morning, Miss Rowan. May I ask how you intended to spend your afternoon before meeting your companion? Or shall I get my head bitten off for my curiosity?"

"I wanted to explore the walled city particularly. I've only had a mere glimpse of it yet."

The sardonic gleam in his eyes gave place to something

more like approval. "Yes, that's always worth while. If I had the time to spare, I'd offer to come with you and guide you, but no doubt that would make me very unpopular both with you and your boy-friend."

Jacynth was amazed at this sudden shift of mood. She was also aware of how much she would have welcomed his offer as escort around the old town. He did not mean it, of course; the suggestion was thrown out idly on the spur of the moment. She realised that she was gripping the edge of the table in front of her, for her legs needed support. He had no right to look at her like that and send her into a world of delight with his insincere suggestions.

"Then may I have the afternoon off, as you promised?" she asked, hoping that her voice was not as shaky as it sounded in her own ears.

"By all means," he agreed. "I don't want a martyr sitting here for the rest of the day." He chuckled. "I was only teasing you."

She turned away, unable to face him any longer. He had incited her to a pitch of anger where she had almost lost her temper. Then, with blandness itself, he admitted that he was only making fun of her.

It was fortunate that after a moment or two, he went out of the room, taking a bundle of documents and files with him.

When Caterina served lunch, Jacynth mentioned that she would not be home for dinner.

The housekeeper clucked with annoyance. From the quickly spoken words, Jacynth gathered that Caterina was furious because there would be no one left to cook for, except herself and her husband. Evidently Mallory was not intending to dine at home, and Jacynth could not ignore her own curiosity about where and with whom he might be spending the evening. The lovely Hermione? Or merely a boring business engagement?

An hour or so later Jacynth was glad to be free from the Villa Kalakos. It would not be true to say it was a prison, but she had not been used to a residential post and apart from that,

Mallory's constant nearness, his dominant maleness had a claustrophobic effect on her.

She walked along the elegant boulevards and shopping streets, relying on the street map for direction that would bring her to one of the gates of the old town.

She found the Palace of the Grand Masters easily enough and spent a long time exploring the expertly restored old building with its grand staircase and the statues in each archway.

At one time she attached herself to a group of people and listened to their courier explaining the history of the hostelries of the Crusaders. Later, she wandered along the Street of the Knights, sensing the mystery and charm of the old buildings.

With a smile, she wondered what it would have been like if Mallory had been her escort and guide today. She was sure he would have been totally different from Ray, whose interest lay more in the direction of pottery, leather and souvenirs in the shops.

If Mallory were half Greek, as she had been told – and she could have guessed that from his features – he would, at least, have some regard for the heritage of the old Greek civilisation.

She was intrigued by the Suleiman Mosque, its dome and minaret dominating one of the main streets, Sokratous, and was fortunate in finding it open. She took off her shoes, leaving them outside in the porch, and entered this ancient building, conscious that it was only in comparatively recent years that women had been allowed to set foot on the carpeted ground floor in the form of a cross. Her glance rose to the latticed balcony where women had sat, segregated from the male congregation below.

Perhaps Greek men, too, such as Mallory Brendon, still retained this Oriental doctrine of the complete superiority of his sex.

But she fended off these intruding thoughts. She had come out today to escape from routine work and routine suppositions about Mallory.

She sat outside a café facing the old Byzantine church and watched several cats stalking birds and each other among the tangled shrubberies of the church grounds. When she had finished her coffee, she wandered around the narrow streets, noticing one or two old houses that had retained their latticed windows. The soaring fronds of a palm tree rose behind the roof of a grocer's shop, and when she came across old fountains in small squares she tried to imagine the gatherings of the town's inhabitants during the Turkish occupation which had lasted for nearly four hundred years.

When she walked through an arched gateway towards the harbour she found that she was not far from the mole where three windmills stood, almost identical with the one in the garden of Kalakos. Only the spokes remained on the axis of each, and Jacynth noticed that when the mills had operated, they all faced the same way and the sails had been fixed in one position. She was puzzled by this oddity, for surely the right wind couldn't always blow from one direction.

In due course she appeared at the Café Actaeon a few minutes before seven o'clock, but almost immediately Ray was standing by her chair.

"*Kalispera!*" they greeted each other, and Ray took both her hands in his as he sat down.

"At last!" he exclaimed. "So the old brute let you out after all! Why couldn't he have given you the evening off last night? Where did you go, by the way? Have you started living it up with your boss?"

Jacynth laughed. "Too many questions! I don't know which to answer first. Well, last night I had to go with Mr. Brendon to a conference at one of the hotels farther along the coast."

She thought that was reasonably near the truth. In order to divert Ray's attention from her own occupations, she asked with a show of eagerness, "What was the exciting news you wanted to tell me?"

Ray adopted a haughty attitude, folding his arms and trying to look stern. "You must wait, my girl. You made me wait since last night, so now it's my turn to keep you guessing." He signalled to a waiter and ordered drinks for Jacynth and himself. "We'll go and eat later, if that suits you?" he suggested.

When she nodded agreement, he leaned forward towards her, his eyes alight with enthusiasm. "You remember I had to go back to Athens a few days ago? Well, I think I've managed to grab quite a nice little job for myself. You see, I made various friends on my previous trip and this time I've looked them up. To cut a long story short, I'm going to launch out on my own as an exporter of Greek goods, instead of being not much more than an errand boy working for a pittance for an English firm."

Jacynth wrinkled her brow. "I don't quite get the idea. You're going into business for yourself? Doesn't that need a large amount of capital?"

Ray shook his head confidently. "Not the way I can work it. Oh, I have a little money of my own and I think I could borrow a bit more from my parents, but as an agent, I don't really have to pay out for the goods at the time. I fulfil the orders from England and other countries, Germany, France, Sweden and so on, and the firms who buy pay through the banks the suppliers here in Greece. I take my substantial commission. No risk at all."

Ray leaned back, making a tent of his fingertips, as though he were already a chairman of an important board.

"And what about the firm you work for now? The one in Bristol, I think you said."

"Oh, I shall have to go back and just tell them that I've better prospects. Too bad I have to ditch them, because probably they may not be inclined to give me any orders at first, but afterwards, they'll find that I'm a first-class agent they can't afford to ignore and they'll come running to eat out of my hand."

When the waiter brought the glasses of wine that Ray had ordered, Jacynth raised hers towards her companion.

"I wish you very good luck," she said. "I suppose you'll be based in Athens."

"Well, I have to arrange with someone I know there to share his office for a time, so that I have an address. Then as soon as I can find somewhere suitable and can afford the rent, I'll launch out with my own establishment. I'd like to get hold of a place with living accommodation above, a small flat — something like that."

"Well, it all sounds very promising," was Jacynth's comment.

"Promising?" he echoed. "Your enthusiasm is overwhelming. I thought you'd be really delighted. Don't you see, my dear Jacynth, that I'll be here permanently in Greece — either Athens or Crete or here in Rhodes? We'll be able to see each other far more often than if I were only on a three-week tour at a time."

"Of course I see that," she returned, but she still could not infuse total delight into her voice. "And it will all be very pleasant."

"For both of us, I hope," he added. "There's another side of it, too. When I get properly fixed up and make the contacts I expect, I might even be able to offer you a job. You'd find me a better boss than that old slave-driver you're working for now."

Jacynth laughed gently. "I'll bear that in mind, but I'm not inclined to throw myself out of one post before I'm sure of another. I can't go on the dole here. I'm a foreigner."

She had not told Ray that at present she was still on trial where Mallory Brendon was concerned and now that Ray had disclosed his own future plans, she saw that it would be foolish to hand him that advantage. He would probably try to persuade her that a secure job with him was infinitely better than uncertainty with Mallory.

"But you wouldn't really prefer to work for him if I could offer you a job?" Ray pursued.

"Perhaps it's rather soon to be discussing such vague prospects," she said with a smile. She had no wish to wound Ray's feelings or undermine his self-confidence, but he seemed inclined to take too much for granted.

After a pause during which he shuffled his feet and his face wore an extremely sulky expression, she suggested, "No doubt you'd be able to extend your territory and do business in Turkey?"

"Oh, I've thought of that." He was all smiles again. "There are tremendous possibilities on the Greek mainland and all the islands and all along the Turkish coast. It's best to start with the coastal towns until you can organise transport from the inland places."

He continued discussing his plans for expansion and Jacynth listened attentively, knowing that he needed an audience. Privately she considered that unless he could raise considerable capital, some of his ideas were quite beyond possibility in the near future. Ray was blowing up vast bubbles to form his dream empire.

He took her to dinner at a small restaurant facing a square and insisted on buying champagne to celebrate his future success.

"I'm sorry that on this tour I really haven't had as much time to spare as I thought I might. We could have gone on several trips here and there and I'd have taken you to one of the pottery places. Even when I've been free, that old slave-driver of yours has put his foot down and prevented you from joining me. But never mind, darling, when I come back in a few weeks' time, we'll remedy that."

Jacynth smiled and nodded tacit acceptance of these future delights.

"When do you return to England?" she asked.

"In four or five days' time. I have to go to Crete again, but I shall come back here before I go on to Athens." He flashed her a quick smile across the table. "I can't forgo the chance of seeing you again."

After the long, leisurely meal Ray suggested that a visit to a night club would be a suitable finish to the evening.

"I doubt if you've had a chance to see anything of Rhodes' night-life. Your boss is hardly likely to take you out and about."

"We shan't be home too late, I hope?" queried Jacynth, remembering that Caterina or Nikon would have to let her in, unless, of course, Mallory happened to be standing in the doorway watching her homecoming, as on that previous occasion.

"Not to worry," replied Ray airily. "You're not a child to be ordered home by ten o'clock."

The café to which he conducted her was in a dark side street, although a flashing sign proclaimed its name, *I Froàola*, which she translated as The Strawberry.

"Odd name for a night-club, isn't it?" she commented with a smile, as she and Ray were ushered through doors, a passage and a flight of stairs down to a smoke-laden room crowded almost to suffocation.

In one corner a *bouzoukia* orchestra tried to make itself heard above the din, and half a dozen couples were trying to dance in a space the size of an average dining table.

Ray managed to find places in a corner and Jacynth squeezed beside him. The fleeting thought brushed her consciousness that if her escort had been Mallory and the crush forced her to sit close beside him, her reaction would have been quite different. As it was, the close contact with Ray made no more impression on her than the nearness of a fellow-traveller in a bus.

Ray ordered ouzo when he could attract the attention of a waiter, although Jacynth would have preferred a soft drink or a glass of light wine.

"I've really drunk enough already with all that champagne," she murmured, but apparently Ray did not hear.

When the drinks came, she splashed a large amount of water into her glass and watched the spirit turn cloudy.

A quartet of Greek dancers in regional costumes began their performance, and Jacynth forgot the lack of comfort and the thick, heavy atmosphere of the room. She noticed that the two men energetically leaped and twisted and stamped, while the women remained gracefully static.

When the performance ended, several young men took the

floor and clumsily copied the movements of the men dancers, making a grotesque parody accompanied by laughter and shouting.

Jacynth was not particularly amused by these capers and was about to suggest to Ray that it was time to leave, when he suddenly spotted someone he knew on the far side of the room.

"Won't be a second. Someone I've been wanting to talk to," he muttered, and threaded his way through the crowds.

Jacynth idly watched as he approached a stout man in shirt sleeves. A few moments later her arm was roughly grasped and she was pulled to her feet.

"You dance?" invited the young man, a dark, hawk-nosed individual, as he thrust his face close to her own.

She tried to pull away, but his friends cleared a pathway and cheered him on. Then she twisted her arm out of his grasp. "Pardon me, but I am English and I don't want to dance," she said in English, not trusting her shaky Greek, in case she made some ludicrous mistake. The young man, her would-be partner, first looked astonished, then accepted the situation and bowed gravely to her with profuse apologies.

Fortunately Ray returned and queried genially, "Anyone annoying you?"

"Not really," she answered, "but if you don't mind, I'd like to leave now."

"Already?" His eyebrows went up. "But we've only just come."

"We've been here some time and – and I've a headache."

"Oh, all right," he grunted.

Out in the street he said, "I thought you'd enjoy the place, unless, of course, you're so sophisticated that such humbler places don't appeal to you."

"It wasn't that, Ray. It was so hot and crowded and stuffy – and I didn't really want to dance with strangers."

"No, I can understand that," he conceded.

Jacynth's private opinion was that Ray should not have deserted her in such circumstances. Would Mallory have done so? But then he would probably never have taken her to a night club at all, let alone a noisy one in a back street.

The night air was fresh and Jacynth was quite prepared to walk back to the Villa Kalakos, but Ray hailed a passing taxi.

In the next few minutes she wished that she had insisted on walking, for Ray took her in his arms and kissed her with more vigour than skill or tenderness.

"You mustn't be cold to me, darling Jacynth," he murmured. "I'm terribly glad I met you that day at the airport, and when I come back and start on my new career, we can have lots of fun together."

"You'll need all your time for your business."

"I can always spare time for a bewitching girl like you." He released her, but kept his arm around her waist and held her close to him. "Besides, you may need a friend like me on the island. I can do you quite a lot of good, one way and another – tell you where to buy anything you want, introduce you to friends who'll give you a discount – that sort of thing. And of course, you won't forget what I said about working for me, will you?"

"No, I won't forget," she assured him, "but I'd hate to leave my present job after so short a time."

The taxi had arrived at the villa and Jacynth alighted quickly. "Don't come up to the door with me. In any case, you'll need the taxi to take you home."

She avoided his would-be lingering good-night kisses, thanked him for a pleasant evening and hurried through the iron gate and up the path to the villa, hoping that the door would not be bolted. It was shut, but Caterina came promptly in answer to the clanging bell that reverberated through the hall when Jacynth pulled the large black knob at the side of the door.

The girl apologised for her late homecoming, but Caterina smiled and murmured that it did not matter. Jacynth noticed as she climbed the stairs that Caterina did not lock and bolt the door, so evidently Mallory was still out somewhere.

Jacynth had only just reached the landing when she heard the sound of the car. She waited, peering over the rail, and very shortly she heard Mallory's voice talking to Caterina, no doubt telling her to lock up. But Jacynth caught a few words that sounded like "Is the English miss in?" and Caterina's affirmative answer.

Jacynth waited no longer, but scuttled off to her bedroom, thanking her lucky stars that she had arrived home even a few minutes before Mallory.

As she undressed and showered she realised how glad she was that Ray was not yet permanently working in Rhodes. Oh, it was pleasant and, indeed, useful to have an English friend here, if only to relieve the nervous edginess that Mallory so often caused in her, but Ray Gurney was not exactly the type of young man she would have chosen.

As she slipped into bed, she allowed her mind to dwell idly on what type she would have selected. There was only one other man with whom she was acquainted and it was plainly ridiculous to imagine Mallory Brendon acting as a companionable escort.

"Well, did you enjoy your jaunt?" he enquired next morning when she was already at work in her office.

"Yes, thank you, very much. I was able to do some sightseeing by myself first before I met Ray. I wandered about in the old town and then by the harbour where the three windmills still stand. But why did they always face the same way? The spokes of the sails seem fixed."

Mallory, on the opposite side of the table, rested his chin on one hand. "Because the prevailing wind always blew from one direction."

"What if it changed?"

"Very rarely. You're not in England now where the winds swing from one point of the compass to another like an unpredictable woman."

Jacynth bent her head towards the long foolscap sheets by her typewriter. "I see. Yes, thank you." Why did he have to twist a simple innocuous question into a personal gibe?

Why, too, did he have to look at her like that so that she was quite powerless to stop the colour flooding up into her face?

For the next quarter of an hour he appeared to be studying various documents and making alterations. Then, without looking up, he asked abruptly, "How long does your boy-friend expect to be here in Rhodes?"

"Only a few days more. He has to return to Athens and then back to England."

"You'll miss him." Mallory's voice sounded sardonic. Jacynth refused to be provoked into a reply one way or the other.

"What does he do for a living? I take it he wasn't just here on holiday?"

This time she looked up and faced him. "No, he wasn't on holiday, but I think you wouldn't expect me to disclose his business connections – any more than I would talk to strangers about yours."

Mallory looked across at her, a light in his dark eyes that might have been approval or perhaps only surprise.

"Your discretion is admirable. I'm glad you have such a sense of responsibility."

Jacynth disliked his taunting tone of voice, but she let it pass.

Then he continued, "Have you wondered why I insist on dictating all my work to my secretary instead of using a tape-machine or some other modern gadget?"

"Yes, I have. It would save a great deal of your time."

"No doubt, but it would also provide my rivals with possible sources of information."

"Your rivals?" she echoed. "I understood you were in a class of your own, way ahead of anyone else in your sphere."

She reddened again as the implication of her words struck her, but now he laughed.

"Even in my sphere, as you call it, one needs security. Also, as you've probably noticed, there is only one telephone in my study, with no extensions anywhere in the house."

"But if people were really determined to learn your secret operations, what is there to stop them from breaking in and stealing the documents, or even photographing them on micro-film?"

Mallory laughed as he looked at her and she noticed how the hard lines of his face softened in relaxation. "You've been seeing too many spy films."

"Not true. I rarely go to the cinema."

"You spend your spare time watching television?"

"Some of it," she answered. "I like reading, listening to music. Sometimes I make a dress."

"Do you play any musical instrument?" he queried.

"Only the piano, and that not really very well. I tried to learn the violin, but I made the most hideous noises that even I couldn't stand it, let alone the neighbours." She laughed at the memory of a neighbour's dog who always set up a tremendous howling every time Jacynth put bow to strings.

"You must entertain me with your piano-playing one evening when we have leisure." Then, without warning, he suddenly rose, slammed down the bundle of documents in his hand and muttered, "You've plenty of work to do now." Then he went out of the room as though a devil were pursuing him.

For a moment or two Jacynth stared at the closed door as though she expected Mallory to materialise through its dark polished panels. Why did he act so strangely? He had started the conversation, first about Ray, then about his own security measures, and somehow the topic had drifted to her own methods of spending her time. What was so odd in that? She racked her brains for anything she had said to cause him to stampede out of her presence with a mumbled command to get back to work. But what was the use of searching for motives where Mallory was concerned? He was entirely unpredictable, even more so than what he regarded as the typical "unpredictable woman". In any case, Mallory would not be disconcerted by anything she could say or do, for he was too impervious to the reactions of other people.

Three days later during the afternoon, Caterina came into Jacynth's office with a message that a young man had called and wanted to see her.

"His name?" queried Jacynth, realising with a sinking heart that her caller could be only Ray.

Caterina tilted her face upwards, raised her eyebrows and clicked her tongue. By now Jacynth had learned, after much confusion, that this was a Greek way of saying "No" and comparable to the English method of shaking the head.

She went out into the hall and Ray came eagerly towards her.

"Can't stop more than a minute. I'm on my way to the airport, but I had to break my journey to see you once more." He put a small parcel into her hands. "This is a little gift, so that you can remember me until I come back."

"Oh, thank you." Jacynth raised a delighted face towards Ray. "I'm sure it will be something I've wanted."

At that moment Mallory came along the wide passage from his study and Jacynth had no choice but to introduce the two men.

"Glad to meet you," acknowledged Ray in his most breezy manner. "I've heard quite a lot about you and how you keep poor Jacynth's nose to the grindstone."

"Indeed!" Mallory's tone was ice itself.

"Ray is on his way to the airport," broke in Jacynth hurriedly before Ray could make any further damaging remarks.

"Then let me wish you *bon voyage*," returned Mallory, whose cold attitude appeared to have deflated Ray to some extent.

"Well then, yes, I must be getting along," said the latter. Then to Jacynth's dismay, he bent towards her, put both arms around her shoulders and gave her a kiss that was no mere goodbye peck, but a full-bodied salute on the lips, obviously aware that he had a definite advantage over a man standing by and looking on.

Jacynth disengaged herself as quickly as she could.

"Goodbye, Ray," she muttered.

"Not goodbye, but *au revoir*." Ray cast an oblique glance at Mallory. "And don't forget, Jacynth, what I said about – about your future prospects."

It was Mallory who moved towards the front door to show Ray out, superficially a courteous action, but Jacynth understood only too readily the real significance.

Still clutching her parcel from Ray, she returned to her office, hoping that Mallory would not follow, but he was close behind her.

"An affectionate young man," he said. "On very good terms with you, apparently. Young people are fast workers these days. So he's coming back to Greece? For a long time?"

"I don't know," muttered Jacynth despairingly. She would have given a great deal for Mallory not to have witnessed that little scene in the hall. Why did Ray have to come at that moment to say his farewells?

"He spoke about *your* future prospects," continued Mallory incisively. "Does that mean you're tying yourself up with his future? You're going to marry him?"

"Oh, no!" exclaimed Jacynth, shocked at this relentless questioning and horrified at the rapid conclusions he was making – or pretending to make.

Mallory's dark eyebrows rose in surprise. "You're not one of those women who prefer to dispense with marriage?"

"No, no, I didn't mean that at all. You're twisting my words." She was nearly in tears.

"Perhaps you'd better open your parting gift, even if it's only a temporary parting," he suggested. She looked up at him and saw the amused smile on his lips, the baiting gleam in his eyes. "Whatever is inside may restore your tranquillity. Obviously his departure has upset you."

"It's nothing of the kind," she flared out at him. "It's you and your incessant questioning. You won't even allow me to have one friend outside this house. You have to pry into everything, even this little present." She stopped in utter confusion, aware that her voice had risen about an octave. "I'm sorry," she mumbled. "I shouldn't have –"

"Why not?" he demanded. "You're quite right. I've no authority to poke my nose into your private affairs." He put his hand over her wrist in what perhaps he intended as a gesture of apology, but the effect on her was anything but assuagement, for her heart was racing, her throat dry and every nerve in her body was tautened almost to the disaster of breaking point.

She sank into her chair. "If you're so keen to know what Ray has given me, I'll open it." She tried to keep her voice steady, but knew she had not succeeded any more than she could control her trembling fingers as she untied the string.

Then, surprisingly gently, he took the parcel out of her hands, unwrapped the paper and stood the two small replicas of Grecian vases on the table. They were black with figures in relief outlined in jade green. One represented a procession of women with urns or vases; the other a slender young man with an elaborate headdress.

"Knossos," murmured Mallory. "You haven't been to Crete yet, I suppose?"

"No. This is my first visit to Greece."

"Then you must certainly visit Crete and especially Knossos for the ruins of the old Minoan civilisation. These little vases are representations of the frescoes. One is the Cup-bearers, the other, this handsome young man, is the Prince of the Lilies."

While he talked, she realised he was giving her time to calm herself.

"These are very poor specimens of pottery," he continued. "I think your boy-friend could have found better samples than these."

"He's probably a very good judge of the qualities of Greek pottery, since he happens to be in that trade and buys stuff here to send to England." Too late, she realised that she had been over-ready to defend Ray and his choice of gift, for now she had disclosed his occupation.

"Oh? So that's what he does. Then all I can say is that he

ships very tawdry consignments to your country, if this is a sample."

She glared at him now. "You're implying that he's given me two cheap little pieces because that's all he could afford. And you're right," she added emphatically. "When I receive a gift, I don't try to calculate how much it cost."

"I know." He smiled at her and reduced her yet again to a quivering bundle of nerves. "It's the thought that counts." He was standing so close to her that the sleeve of his jacket brushed her shoulder and she edged a little farther away. She could not endure his nearness, his magnetic presence that seemed to draw her irrevocably towards him.

He was still smiling and she turned her head away.

"You appear to be very distressed at parting from this chap Gurney — I think you said that was his name — and his farewell kisses have had a bad effect on you. Let's see how we can remedy matters and soothe you."

Without warning he jerked her to her feet and swung her into his arms. "Perhaps one of my brand of kisses will compensate." His mouth came down on hers in a long kiss that was hard and angry and demanding, with no tenderness in it. He held her so close that it was impossible for her to pull away, but now she had lost the will to fend him off. He was arousing her to a passion and a desire that she had never experienced before. She wanted his kiss to continue for ever. She felt herself responding, even though a more sensible voice in her brain cried out that it was foolish to do so and surrender to this arrogant man's whim of the moment.

When at last he released her, she grasped the edge of the table for support, for her knees were unsteady. Then she flopped into her chair and dared not look at him.

"H'm, it seems that one man's kiss is as good as another's in your opinion." His voice held a stinging sarcasm which wounded her more than his bruising mouth. "But I suppose most girls of today are the same as you, permissive, even promiscuous."

She was too shaken to find words, then as he was going out

of the door, she said, "Maybe you shouldn't judge other people by your own yardstick."

At the door he paused. "I wonder if you know very much about my particular yardstick."

Then he was gone. She held her head in her hands and let the slow, hot tears fall. What sort of exhibition had she made of herself in these last few minutes? She had betrayed herself into a passionate response that had lain dormant, that she had not even imagined she could feel for one man, let alone Mallory Brendon. Worse than that, she had revealed to him that she wanted him to make love to her.

The thought of David flashed across her troubled mind and she raised her head and stared into space. David? She had imagined herself in love with him, but now she knew beyond doubt that her feeling for him was only a pale misty wraithlike affair lacking substance. She had merely been in love with love.

Now she had to confess to herself that she was in love with a man, a man of overpowering masculine vitality, but one who was not destined for Jacynth. In due time no doubt he would marry Hermione – or even some other girl with a rich father, a marriage of financial interests rather than of love. In the meantime, Jacynth must steel herself to continue working for him as though he were a middle-aged man with a family and not in the least sexually attractive. She would concentrate on the least likeable aspects of his personality; no doubt he had a few faults here and there. He must never guess the state of her true feelings.

Permissive. Promiscuous. Those were the epithets he had applied to her, almost hurled at her when he must have realised that she was in no composed state to reply. Naturally, a man of Mallory's calibre, a man who must realise that he could have almost any woman come running to him, would take the view that every girl who fell for his charms was an easy conquest.

As she resumed her work, Jacynth realised that in the last hour or so, she had left her girlhood behind and become a woman, with all a woman's desires, and aware that love was not all moonlight and roses, but a pathway of thorns accompanied by an unbearable ache for one man and the fulfilment he could give her, but which she would never know.

CHAPTER FIVE

"At the end of the week I intend to go to Lindos," Mallory announced to Jacynth one morning.

"Yes?" She looked up, awaiting further instructions.

"And I want you to come with me."

"Very well," she murmured. As though she had any choice in the matter! As though she would not have accompanied him to the middle of the Sahara or up the Himalayas!

He was frowning over a contract and she forbore to interrupt him. After a few moments she enquired, "Will you be working there? I mean, are we to take the typewriter and so on?"

"What?" He withdrew his attention from the document and stared at her. "Oh, er – no. Probably not."

Her spirits rose foolishly. More than a week had gone by since Ray's departure and that subsequent scene when Mallory had kissed her with such humiliating intensity, and during those intervening days, he had behaved as the business man who was her employer. The trifling episode, which was no doubt how he regarded it, was completely wiped from his memory, apparently.

Now he was proposing a trip to Lindos, the town halfway along the east coast of the island, the place where the ruins of an acropolis dominated a hillside village overlooking the sea. So far Jacynth had not had time to visit it, but she had decided that as soon as time allowed, she would make an expedition. Now, to her delight, Mallory would be taking her.

"We shall be staying there over the week-end," he said, "so take whatever you think necessary – clothes and so on."

"Of course." Already she was reviewing in her mind her not very extensive wardrobe.

"We shall be staying at one of Mr. Perandopoulos's houses." Mallory broke in on her musings. "You remember that you met Miss Perandopoulos, Hermione, at the Summer Palace a week or two ago."

"Yes, I remember." Jacynth had to say something, but her elation had already evaporated. So he was spending the week-end with Hermione at one of her father's villas. Jacynth felt herself reduced to the role of secretarial hanger-on, yet that was absurd, for obviously he was not compelled to take her, and his next words confirmed that view.

"I think we both need a break of a day or two. You've worked hard and I've piled the stuff on to you. I need a little bit of relaxation myself."

Jacynth thought grimly that no doubt in the company of Hermione he would get all the relaxation he needed, but she banished these unworthy ideas.

She listened carefully to Mallory's instructions as to the various documents he required to be given priority.

He turned sharply with a foolscap folder in his hands and the edge caught one of the small Greek vases that Ray had given Jacynth. The Prince of the Lilies lay shattered on the floor.

"Oh, sorry about that." Mallory's tone was no more than perfunctory.

He was not sorry at all, thought Jacynth as she bent to pick up the pieces. He had probably timed his movement most carefully and deliberately to send the vase off the window-ledge.

"I'm afraid it's not possible to mend it," he said. "The clay is too powdery to hold together."

"It doesn't matter," she said woodenly.

"But it does!" he contradicted. "This little pot was precious to you because of the giver. I must buy you another to replace it."

She wrapped the broken fragments in a sheet of paper and thrust them into the wastepaper basket.

He did not really mean what he said about giving her a

replacement. He was probably thinking "Cheap and nasty", the same valuation as he put upon Ray, but Jacynth controlled her temper. The loss of a small piece of pottery was not worth jeopardising a week-end visit to Lindos. If she made a scene, Mallory was quite capable of cancelling his good intention to take her with him.

Later, however, she took the remaining vase, the one with the Cup-bearers, up to her room. There was no sense in providing Mallory with a second target.

On Friday morning Jacynth was up earlier than usual, for it would be a bad start to the week-end if she kept Mallory waiting. She had showered, breakfasted and dressed by half-past seven. She gave a final glance to her new outfit, a dress and jacket of strawberry pink. Matching trousers to wear with the jacket were already packed in her small week-end case, so that she could ring the changes with one or two tops. At home in England she rarely wore hats, but here in Rhodes the spring sun was powerful and now she had a natural colour straw hat with a gracefully curving wide brim to shade her face and prevent her hair from drying and bleaching.

When she went down to the hall, Nikon took her case out to the car. Mallory was already standing by the bonnet. In casual clothes, pale sand-coloured slacks and jacket with cream shirt and a dark green silk tie, he looked younger, and Jacynth had to repress her feelings of delighted excitement at the prospect of this week-end jaunt in his company.

"New dress?" he queried as she approached the car.

"Yes. I bought it here in Rhodes."

Then he spoke in Greek and smiled. "That means 'wear it in good health'. You must always say that when someone appears in new clothes."

"A nice thought," commented Jacynth, wondering if she would ever be able to return that compliment. How would she know when he was wearing anything new? That was something that usually only wives knew.

Sitting next to him in the car was enchanting, but not relaxing, for his nearness troubled her. She was sure that sooner

93

or later he would notice that she was trembling and then ask her for the reason. She controlled herself by gazing out of the window and concentrating on the scenery.

The countryside after they had left the town of Rhodes was a revelation to Jacynth. The road wound through gentle slopes covered with wild flowers. Vast stretches of golden yellow, sheets of mauve, and clusters of blue flowers made a multi-coloured pattern of the fields.

"It's like a flower carpet," she murmured, and was aware of Mallory's quick sideways glance.

"Rhodes is famous for its wild flowers." He slowed the car to a halt where the road was wide enough. "Would you like to see some of the flowers? Are you a good botanist?"

"Not very good," she laughed. She was grateful for any little interlude that indicated Mallory's inclination to forget business problems for a day or two.

In the next few minutes it appeared that Mallory was extremely knowledgeable about flowers, for as he strolled about and picked specimens at random, he identified them for her. "Anemones, marigolds, vetch. Poppies, but not the ordinary English variety. This cyclamen is a local Rhodes special. We have several varieties of flowers that are unique here in Rhodes and grow nowhere else. There's one that comes later, not unlike a clover, but it grows only in a very small area, and then it covers whole fields with its flowers."

When she and Mallory returned to the car, Jacynth carefully wrapped the little posy in a paper tissue and laid it on the back seat. The flowers would quickly wilt and she must try not to read into this insignificant little cluster any deeper meaning because Mallory had taken the trouble to pick the bunch.

Her first view of Lindos was of a village of sparkling white houses nestling at the foot of a rocky promontory crowned by the ruins of the acropolis. To the left lay the deep sapphire of the Aegean Sea and, sheltered by an arm of purple and brown rock, a lagoon of smooth silky water edged with a crescent of sand.

"Before we go up to the Perandopoulos villa," Mallory said, "I want to go the other way and see what progress is being made on the new hotel."

Jacynth hid the smile which curved her lips. Naturally, Mallory would never be able to take a day off without attending to some aspect of business wherever possible.

The new hotel was barely half completed and situated on the curve of the bay where it would have direct access to the beach. It had not yet been given a name, but was known to Jacynth as "Project L.201" meaning that it would have two hundred rooms and that it was the first part of a complex that would include blocks of apartments, restaurants, and the indispensable swimming pool.

Mallory had already explained to her that in his opinion the enormous multi-storey blocks of hotels were no longer popular.

"Tourists are beginning to realise that they feel insignificant in the colossal structures. Oh, at first, they liked the immense size, the huge restaurants and all that, but now the trend is towards smaller hotels linked together in the same grounds, everything spread out, more elbow room."

"As long as the land is cheap?" queried Jacynth.

"Certainly, the site must be comparatively inexpensive, although that's the least of our problems."

Now, as he and Jacynth toured the site, stepping over planks and skirting piles of drainpipes, she saw the value of his argument. A vast bulk of masonry would have spoilt the proportion of the surroundings, a "blot on the landscape", it would probably have been termed, but this four-storey hotel with its curved façades would fit into the background, making use of the pines and cypress trees left undisturbed.

The swimming pool had already been excavated and constructed, but was not yet tiled. Mallory spoke to several men whom Jacynth took to be foremen or supervisors and sometimes they unrolled plans or diagrams smudged with thumbmarks, grease-spots or even wine stains.

"Everything seems to be going according to plan," was

Mallory's comment when he and Jacynth returned to his car and were on their way to their destination.

She speculated if that phrase "according to plan" would also apply to the whole week-end.

Hermione greeted her guests in the courtyard of a white villa situated on a small rise of land so that it overlooked the lagoon and the sea beyond. She was wearing a brilliant emerald silk trouser suit, the tunic in Chinese mandarin style richly embroidered and open in the front down to the waist where it was held by a large brooch of twisted gold.

"How late you are!" she greeted Mallory, extending both hands towards him. To Jacynth she gave a mere nod of acknowledgment, and the girl wondered if Hermione had been aware that Mallory was not coming alone.

"I see you've brought your new secretary with you," Hermione said icily. "I hope that doesn't mean you intend to work all the time you're here."

"No, indeed," Mallory hastened to assure her. "I've brought Jacynth to enjoy a glimpse of part of the island. She's had little chance to go exploring."

"Jacynth?" echoed Hermione. "An unusual name."

Jacynth suspected that Hermione's remark was triggered off not by an unusual Christian name, but because Mallory had used it so casually and the knowledge had a curiously warming effect on her.

"Besides, who knows?" continued Mallory with a malicious gleam in his eyes, "I might have sudden inspirations that will rock the world of finance and then I should need my secretary at the ready."

"Then we shall all hope that your brain will not function at all during the week-end more than to let you swim in the pool or lounge about the garden and eat the meals cooked by our new French chef." Hermione linked her arm in Mallory's and began to stroll towards the house. "Incidentally, my father is away and may not be back for a few days, so you'll have no excuse to talk to him."

Jacynth was shown to a room with a breathtaking view of

azure sea and lighter blue sky and between the house and sea edge the multi-colour rocks, purple, grey, green and yellow as the sun caught the rough surfaces.

From here she could see the narrow entrance to the lagoon rom the sea between a cliff that rose sheer on one side and a sharp point of rock on the other. Only comparatively small vessels could negotiate that inlet, yachts, small boats, but certainly no steamers.

Lunch was served on a shady verandah and the attendants outnumbered those eating, for so far Mallory and Jacynth appeared to be the sole guests. The food was deliciously French, beginning with Vichyssoise and ending with fairy light mille-feuilles, so evidently the new chef promised success.

In reply to Mallory's query as to who else was expected, Hermione gave a little laugh, lowered her eyelids and then smartly snapped wide-open eyes at the man opposite. "I'm sorry if you expected a party of guests here," she said demurely. "No one else is coming – unless, of course, someone drops in."

Jacynth kept her attention fixed on her plate. So Hermione had been expecting Mallory alone. Naturally, she was disappointed now not to have him entirely to herself for the next couple of days, but no doubt Jacynth could make herself scarce when the occasion demanded.

"Suits me," agreed Mallory. "I dislike having to make small talk to people I hardly know." He paused and his next sentence jerked Jacynth not only to awareness, but to alarm. "Then I'll be able to take Jacynth around and show her the sights of Lindos."

Jacynth's fleeting glance at Hermione caught the fiery gleam of anger in the latter's hazel eyes, quickly veiled, but the pout still lingered on that luscious mouth.

"And I suppose I am to stay at home and while away my time as best I can." She leaned her elbows on the table and the opening of her mandarin tunic fell apart to reveal the curves of her full breasts. Jacynth saw Mallory's gaze dwell on Her-

97

mione's seductive charms, then he turned his head sharply away.

"Or I could provide you with picnic lunches," Hermione continued smoothly, but with a definitely cutting edge to her voice. "Or would it be more discreet if I acted as chaperone?"

Jacynth's face flamed at the innuendo and now she was resentful of Mallory's carelessly-chosen words. Why had he brought her here if she was to be the target of Hermione's spiteful remarks?

But in the next instant she suspected that Mallory was teasing and baiting the beautiful Greek girl just the same as he provoked every other woman. She decided that it was not her place to take part in this kind of conversation and was thankful when Mallory started a different topic.

All the same, as she and Mallory were the only guests, Jacynth felt keenly that she was the intruder. Later in the afternoon, Mallory suggested he would swim in the pool.

"What about you, Jacynth? Brought your bikini?"

"No. I wasn't sure if anywhere would be warm enough to swim."

"Our pool is heated to any temperature we want," put in Hermione.

"No doubt Hermione can find you something to swim in," suggested Mallory, turning towards Jacynth. "You do swim, I suppose?"

"Yes, adequately, but not expertly."

As one would probably expect, by the side of the swimming pool there were elaborate changing cabins with showers, dressing tables provided with cosmetics and perfumed sprays. Jacynth found a selection of bikinis and a towelling wrap waiting for her when she tentatively chose one of the cabins.

She chose a flowered blue and white bikini, donned the wrap and emerged to find that Mallory was already in the water while Hermione stood on the steps, adopting a pose that she must have known enhanced her lovely figure. She wore a petunia colour one-piece suit and Jacynth thought with a touch of mild envy that Hermione certainly knew how to magnify her own charms. Not for her the two-piece that cut a feminine body in half, but the single garment, low-cut and almost backless, that hugged the flowing lines of her body.

Jacynth entered the water with a slightly ungainly, splashing jump and swam to the end of the pool which was shaped roughly like a figure eight with a narrow part in the middle. She turned and swam on her back, but when she reached the narrow section, she felt two hands placed on either side of her head.

"Please not to struggle or you will drown," Mallory had adopted a ludicrous accent in a high-pitched voice.

Jacynth was so unnerved by this unexpected contact which sent her heart thudding wildly that she let her body double like a jack-knife and promptly sank. After a moment's floundering she came up gasping and laughing, but now Mallory was innocently sitting on the edge of the pool, his arms folded across his chest, his legs dangling in the water.

"You are in difficulties?" he asked politely in his normal voice.

"Not at all!" she answered. "Someone seemed to think I was in need of life-saving, but he pushed me under."

"I'm told that in this pool there lurks an evil spirit fond of horseplay, especially with girl swimmers."

Jacynth laughed, but the little scene was immediately interrupted by the arrival of Hermione, who had walked along the tiled rim of the pool.

"You promised to teach me to dive better," she said now to Mallory. "Come, we must practise."

For the next quarter of an hour, Jacynth watched the diving lesson. Mallory, a lean figure in black trunks, would swoop into the water like a diving bird, then Hermione would advance to the end of the platform, apparently summon up her courage and launch herself into the water. Then Mallory would next time adjust the girl's arm position or clasp her waist to alter her balance. The sight of this handsome couple, Mallory, tanned no doubt from previous summers, and Hermione, a contrast with her creamy skin against his darker one, eventually became more than Jacynth could bear and she strolled away to the opposite end of the pool. But she could not shut out from her inner vision the picture of Mallory embracing Hermione in a variety of ways.

Jacynth plunged into the water for a final swim, then climbed out and ran to the changing cabin for a towel to dry her hair.

Dinner was served in an elegantly furnished room with ornate mirrors reflecting the candelabra on the table. Jacynth felt that Mallory should not have brought her here where she was so obviously *de trop*, unless he had some secret purpose of his own. After dinner when Mallory and Hermione played backgammon, Jacynth knew that this game had been deliberately chosen by Hermione, for backgammon is not a game that three can share.

As soon as she could do so, she excused herself and retired to her bedroom, to read for a while, but not to relax in peace, for she was tortured by her own imagination. Mallory and Hermione in each other's arms? Mallory kissing Hermione with infinite tenderness and murmuring words of love?

When at last she went to bed, Jacynth wished heartily that Mallory had left her behind at the Villa Kalakos with only Caterina and Nikon for company. The long dreary week-end stretched before her like a desert.

When she appeared next morning after breakfasting on her balcony, Mallory came towards her. "Are you ready to come exploring in Lindos?"

"Why, yes, of course," she replied. "Now?"

"Naturally."

"I think I should change my shoes," she suggested, regarding her white sandals. "Something stronger, perhaps."

"Then don't be half an hour," he warned her.

She raced up to her room, kicked off the sandals, put on a pair of beige suede shoes with thick soles, decided that the strawberry pink trousers and white polo-neck jumper would be suitable, and was down in the hall inside five minutes. She had no idea if Hermione was to accompany Mallory, but

Jacynth was not going to dally and lose the chance of a morning sightseeing with him.

To her delight, she and Mallory set off alone. There was no sign of Hermione, but when Jacynth turned to look back at the villa, she believed she could see her hostess standing on a balcony.

"We could easily take a shorter way up to the Acropolis," Mallory explained as she walked beside him along a path that led downwards instead of ascending to the top of the hill, "but I think you should see the village nearer sea level. That way you'll get a better impression of how the Acropolis dominates the place, and it's always more interesting to walk about at street level than to look down on a medley of houses from above."

"Oh, yes, I quite agree," she returned happily.

"Are you strong? It's a fair climb right up to the top."

"I'm not an old lady who needs a walking stick," she retorted mildly.

She was aware of his quick sideways glance. "Not yet," was his sardonic rejoinder. "Although, of course, for the lame and the infirm, there are donkeys to take you to the top."

"Poor donkeys," she murmured. "I've already seen the loads the poor animals have to carry." Along the track to the left half a dozen donkeys were burdened with fat women and heavyweight men.

"Don't be so intolerant of old age," he rebuked her. "How would you relish it if you were seventy instead of twenty and deprived of the pleasures of seeing antiquities unless some simple form of transport were available?"

Jacynth laughed. "I suppose it's because at my age it's practically impossible to imagine what one would be like in old age. Even fifty seems very elderly."

"Thank you," he said, bridling. "I have less than twenty years then before I become a doddering old man crippled with rheumatism and – "

"Please, Mr. Brendon!" She had nearly called him "Mallory" because that was the way she thought of him. "Don't twist all my words every time. I'm sure that when you are long past fifty you'll still be as energetic and vigorous as you are now."

And probably even more arrogant and self-willed, she added in her mind.

"Where have you learned the art of flattery?" he demanded.

She hesitated a moment or two before replying. "I wasn't trying to flatter you, just correcting a wrong impression."

He gave a little grunt. "You've probably had quite a lot of practice on your previous bosses or chiefs, but I assure you that I'm totally allergic to honeyed words."

"I understand," she said quietly. Unless the "honeyed words" were spoken by Hermione, perhaps?

"You've probably noticed that all the houses in the village are similar." He stopped in a tiny square to point out to her the uncompromising square houses with flat roofs. "All must be whitewashed and the shutters painted brown. So if someone picks up some tins of mauve or pink paint, it's no use trying to be individual. And no skyscrapers, as you see. In fact, there's very strict supervision on the buildings here. All plans must be passed by the town architectural society."

"But you have the new hotel being built farther along the bay."

"Yes, and that's exactly why it is farther along the bay, although it's not high and, we hope, blends with the background. Even then, we had plenty of difficulties."

"Did Mr. Perandopoulos have his villa built or buy it from someone else?"

"No, he chose the site and had it built two or three years ago, but even he had to submit to the local planning people. Not that he'd worry about one particular house in a small town in Rhodes. He has at least eight or ten establishments of one sort or another in different parts of Europe. One in the West Indies, I think and, of course, an apartment in New York."

Jacynth became interested in some of the small shops that sold souvenirs, pottery or rugs and scarves and at one house she found she could peer into the dark interior and watch two women actually at work on looms.

"I'd advise that we stop here on the way down," came Mallory's voice in her ear, as she stood there absorbed in the weaving process. "Otherwise, I may never get you up to the summit."

She turned quickly towards him with a smile and was again disturbed by the intent look in his dark eyes. She wrenched her gaze away from his face and stepped smartly along the path.

"You're quite right," she said. "One must reach the objective first and dawdle afterwards."

"A cryptic remark," he muttered, "but I'm not going to ask what you meant."

The ascending paths had been made easy for tourist climbers, with many shallow steps and on the grass at the sides, women and children displayed lace mats and embroidered traycloths. Eventually the path became rougher and Jacynth was glad when at one point there was a large plateau shaded with ficus trees. Here, an enterprising café-owner had hauled up a stock of fruit juice in cans and was selling them as fast as he could puncture the tops and insert a straw.

"Would you like a drink?" Mallory asked Jacynth.

"Thank you, I'd love it."

As she gratefully sucked at her straw, Mallory moved towards the rock face where a ship had been carved in stone relief, a galley with billowing sails and many oarsmen.

Jacynth stood looking at it for some time, absorbed in its beauty, until Mallory whispered, "Are you ready for these hundreds of steps.

She nodded and climbed by his side until the ruins of the Acropolis came into view.

"A lot of work has been done here," Mallory explained, "excavating and restoring, although there's a great deal more to be done."

Jacynth gazed with awe on the partly restored Temple of Athena, winging herself back in imagination to the fourth century B.C. when this temple had been in use. She put her hand on the warm stone of the pillars.

"Isn't it a marvellous feeling to be able to touch the stone that other hands shaped and put into position more than two thousand years ago?" she murmured to Mallory.

"Do you get any kind of reaction or vibration?"

"I don't know. I just feel it's a communication by touch, something more than just looking at antiquities. Oh, I know that if we all touched everything, we should ruin the very treasures we've come to see, but perhaps these pillars can endure a few more hands for a few more centuries."

An almost tender smile moved his lips, but was soon replaced by his more usual firm expression.

When they had explored all the ruins, he said, "There's one place here where you can see the most vivid colours in the cliffs that go sheer down."

She accompanied him to the spot he pointed out and saw the bright reds and greens, purple and terra-cotta of the cliff, cut and fissured into a hundred surfaces to expose a different shade.

"I've never seen such wonderful colours," she said, then moved slightly nearer the edge. Immediately Mallory's arm had whipped itself around her waist and pulled her against him with some force.

He released her quickly and as she regained her balance she heard in his voice a note that she had not known before, as he said, "Don't do that again! It's dangerous!"

He spoke truly, for she had certainly rushed into danger; she might have lost her balance or the ground might have crumbled. But the situation had been even more dangerous than the physical one. In that brief moment while his arm held her in a vice-like grip, she had experienced an exultant thrill, and fire had coursed in her veins. In another second or so she would have turned towards him and melted into his arms, hardly caring that the place was public or that bright sunlight revealed the scene.

She was far from calm as she returned with Mallory down the long wide flight of steps to the level below where walls had been reconstructed and Doric columns pieced together. She trod firmly in an effort to quell her racing pulses. Not for worlds would she trip or stumble so that Mallory would be forced to assist her. He would immediately guess that she was stumbling deliberately to invite his help.

On the way down in the village, Mallory stopped at one medieval house. "I think we may be able to look at the courtyard here."

He pushed open an iron gate and guided Jacynth to a square paved with exquisite mosaics, the colours fresh and glowing, the designs intricate and sometimes amusing. Two heroes dressed for war had their glances fixed on the girls they left behind them, a child stooped to scoop a fish from a pond, and someone who was over-ambitious was left dangling on a thin shaky branch of a tree that he had tried to climb.

Afterwards she walked into the house where the two women operated their looms and Jacynth viewed with great pleasure the magnificent rugs and shawls they offered for sale.

"I have a friend who is being married soon," she said to Mallory. "I'd like to send her a present from here. Do you think a rug?"

"Depends on your friend's taste, of course. Actually, you will probably do better here as far as price is concerned than you might in the town."

The prices were clearly marked and when she had made her choice, a fine specimen in black, white and various shades of mauve and purple interwoven, she spoke to Mallory. "I'm afraid my Greek isn't adequate enough to ask about delivery. Would they send it to the villa?"

"The Perandopoulos place? That's hardly worth the trouble. I'll carry it for you."

Jacynth was both astonished and embarrassed by his offer and nervously bit her lip as the woman rolled up the rug, tied it with cord and handed it to Mallory with a string of many good wishes, to which he replied with gracious smiles.

"If the burden becomes too heavy for me," he said to Jacynth when they left the house, "I shall hire a donkey."

This remark relieved her tension and she laughed. "I wasn't so concerned about the sheer weight of the parcel, but – "

"Yes?" he prompted, when she stopped.

"Well, I don't expect my employer to carry my parcels when I go shopping."

"I suppose on previous occasions you carried his?"

She laughed afresh. "I've never accompanied any of my bosses on shopping expeditions."

"Then one must always welcome new experiences."

Today Jacynth found it almost impossible to reconcile Mr. Brendon who at the Villa Kalakos treated her as a typing machine with the man Mallory who was behaving like a lighthearted schoolboy.

Later in the day, however, she discovered that the carefree mood of the morning disappeared on return to the Perandopoulos villa and Hermione. Lunch was a subdued meal with fragmentary conversation and long pauses, during which Hermione sat with her face turned away from Mallory.

Jacynth discreetly retired to her bedroom on pretext of a siesta, undismayed by Hermione's cutting remark, "So Mallory managed to tire you out!"

Evidently the Greek girl had been annoyed because Mallory and Jacynth had gone off to explore Lindos and the ruins without her, but Jacynth could not believe that Mallory as a guest would be so lacking in courtesy as not to have told Hermione last night of his plans.

Or had this morning's outing been decided on the spur of the moment, just when Jacynth appeared?

Well, they would have to fight it out between them, for after an hour Jacynth put on the bikini she had worn yesterday, slipped a cotton dress over it and walked down to the beach of the lagoon. She sat for a while in the shade of the tamarisk trees and gazed at the blue water, the narrow inlet between the rocks through which it was traditionally claimed that the Apostle Paul had sailed to land at Lindos to preach Christianity.

After a while it occurred to her that perhaps she ought not

to have absented herself from the villa as though she were on holiday. Suppose Mallory wanted her for some business purpose?

She decided to swim first in the crystal-clear water and return later to the villa. She was not too sure of the depth of water, so she prudently swam parallel with the shore and when she considered she had been in long enough, she saw Mallory standing on the edge of the water, scanning the beach this way and that. Her first impulse was to turn away and pretend she was not there, but this would no doubt lead eventually to awkward explanations. Besides, he might have some message to give her. She swam into shallow water and waded ashore close to where he was standing, aware that he was watching her, but there was no smile on his face and she wondered exactly what crime she had committed.

"Was it all right for me to come down here?" she asked tentatively.

"Why not?"

She walked the few steps to where she had left her towel and began to mop the droplets of water on her shoulders and arms, her thighs and the slender circle of her waist. He had followed her and stood only inches away from her, and the fact that he did not speak again added to her nervous turbulence. She did not look at him but concentrated on drying herself, rubbing her hair vigorously. Without warning he took the towel from her and began to mop her back. The touch of his fingers through the thick towel made her want to dance up and down for sheer joyousness, and for the second time today she had only to twist her body to fall straight into his embrace. She closed her eyes, giving herself up to the exquisite delight that enveloped her from top to toe, although knowing that his gesture was only on the ordinary level of seaside companionship, where the inhibitions of business life were temporarily waived.

"Dry now, I think," he murmured, unaware that she longed to damp herself all over again for such prolonged pleasure.

To hide her confusion, she sat down abruptly, leaning

against a small upturned boat.

"Too much sun after swimming isn't good for you," he said. "You should sit in the shade."

He pulled her to her feet and, again, his touch on her wrists made her senses reel, but she controlled herself and walked soberly with him to the shelter of one of the straw umbrellas a few yards along the beach.

He sat with his hands clasped around his knees and stared across the sapphire water. "Why did you prefer to come down here to the bay for swimming? Wasn't the pool at the villa large enough?"

She could scarcely confess, "I wanted to leave you and Hermione alone together," so she answered, "Yes, there's more space here."

"You prefer to be a small frog in a large pond rather than the other way round?"

Jacynth smiled. "I hadn't thought of it, but perhaps it's true. I'll leave the big frogs to please themselves."

He turned towards her and she noticed again the straight nose, the high cheekbones and the strong jawline, but most of all his dark eyes, glittering now with amusement, or was it a more challenging expression?

"You count me a big frog?" he demanded.

"How could I answer that question when I've no idea of the size of your pond? I'd assume your area would be the Mediterranean. From a business point of view, I mean," she added hastily.

"You flatter me. Although, as I've already told you, flattery is of no interest to me."

When she remained silent for a moment or two, he said suddenly, "That girl Diana – the one whose place you took. Did she decide suddenly to get married?"

Jacynth shook her head. "I've no idea about that. All I knew was when someone came round collecting for the usual wedding present."

"And her husband? What's his profession?"

"An accountant, I think." Jacynth had only heard the

vaguest details of the man, but perhaps Mallory would be satisfied with such scraps of information as she could give him.

"Canadian? I think you said they'd gone to Canada."

"No. He just had some very good position offered him in Toronto."

Mallory said nothing for a few seconds, then he gave a one-sided smile. "Next time I go to Toronto I must look her up and see if she's done well for herself."

"Is that all that matters?" asked Jacynth impulsively. "That a girl should 'do well for herself' when she marries?"

He turned towards her, his eyes narrowed to slits. "Isn't that what matters to the majority of girls?"

"Surely love must come into it." But Jacynth mumbled the words, having lost her flash of courage and remembering that not only was Mallory her employer and a hard taskmaster at that, but she had completely lost her heart to him. So she was now treading dangerous ground, for never by any slight implication or gesture must he ever suspect the truth.

"Oh, love!" Mallory's hand swept such emotions into the sea. "A certain amount of physical rapture and then the real nub of two people living together with the harmony wearing thinner all the time. In most cases, only a comfortable standard of living can make the whole affair worthwhile. Love in a cottage rarely answers, unless both parties are prepared to make great sacrifices, and surely it's usually the woman who loses most."

Jacynth sighed, hardly knowing whether he was jesting in this cynical manner to disguise his real feelings about Hermione or if his views were sincere.

When she did not speak, he continued, "This young man of yours here in Rhodes – what has he to offer you?"

Perhaps it was safer to veer the conversation towards Ray. "Nothing much at present. He'll need all his capital to start in business on his own."

"Indeed? Launching out as a pottery buyer?"

"Not only pottery," she corrected. "He hopes to act as

agent for many kinds of Greek articles, jewellery, embroideries as well as woven rugs."

"Very ambitious," was Mallory's dry rejoinder. "I must wish him luck."

"He'll probably need it," Jacynth added. She ran a comb through her hair and it flowed in a shining mass around her shoulders. Then she picked up the mini-dress she had worn to come down to the beach, slipped it over her head and stood up. Her fingers were none too steady as she zipped up the front, but she hoped Mallory had not noticed her agitation.

"Yes, we'd better go back," he murmured. "We mustn't completely neglect our hostess."

The Perandopoulos villa was built on several levels to accord with the sloping hillside and a flight of stone steps led from one part of the garden to an upper floor. Mallory conducted Jacynth this way, through an arch to a wide verandah.

Jacynth assumed that only bedrooms were on this floor, but Mallory indicated double doors that led to a large drawing room from which came the sound of animated conversation. Half a dozen people stood or sat in various parts of the room while Hermione reclined on a settee and a handsome young man sat on the floor at her feet.

So Hermione was not at this moment being actually neglected, thought Jacynth. Vague introductions were made by Hermione or Mallory, but Jacynth was eager to slip away at the earliest opportunity, for she was acutely aware of her casual appearance, wearing only a cotton dress over a bikini. In fact, she was not too pleased that Mallory had landed her in here among all these people.

Dressing for dinner, she reflected that a dinner party among strangers would be preferable to the uncomfortable meals at which she had been the embarrassed third, spoiling what should have been a tête-à-tête occasion for Hermione and Mallory.

She put on the best outfit she had, a filmy white blouse embroidered in gold thread and a long skirt patterned with beech brown leaves on a white ground.

She went down to the terrace where she guessed pre-dinner cocktails were being served and met the hostility in Hermione's dark eyes. Jacynth longed for this week-end visit to be over, but there was no escape yet.

CHAPTER SIX

If Hermione had deliberately set out to prove to Jacynth the desperately wide gap that could possibly separate two women, then she could not have accomplished the task more successfully.

Hermione, accustomed to entertaining on the grand scale, moved through the evening, the perfect hostess, wearing a shimmering dress of amber brocade which provided a superb background for her spectacular jewellery. When she turned her head to talk to Mallory on her right at the table, the emerald and diamond necklace scintillated; when she gestured gracefully to the man on her left, bracelets flashed.

There were more than a dozen guests at dinner tonight and Jacynth was seated between two elderly men who spoke very little English. Her attempts to carry on a polite conversation in Greek met with little success, and halfway through the long meal with its many courses they abandoned her and concentrated on their other partners. During a lull, she heard one speaking in French to the lady on his left and was about to tell him that French was her best foreign language and reasonably adequate. Then she heard him say distinctly that he had been landed with a stupid English girl, evidently some poor little waif whom Hermione had befriended.

Jacynth nearly choked on the morsel of fish she was just swallowing. So she was *"une épave"*, was she? A poor little waif brought in and given a square meal! Jacynth naturally remained silent about her ability to talk French, for that disclosure would only embarrass the man and probably amuse the woman beside him.

After dinner she spent the rest of the evening sitting in a dim corner of the terrace. Occasionally a manservant filled her wineglass or asked if she needed anything, but in a way she was glad to be left alone. Here, in the scented darkness with the cypress trees silhouetted vaguely against the star-spattered sky, she was spared the torture of watching Hermione in all her splendour displaying herself as the ideal partner for Mallory. The effect would not be lost on him, and who could blame him if he eventually acknowledged the message?

Jacynth decided that at midnight she would creep away as unobtrusively as possible to her bedroom. No one would notice her comings and goings. She felt a stab of pain at the thought that all during dinner and since, Mallory had not even glanced her way, let alone spoken to her. If he were ashamed of that little waif who was his secretary, why then had he insisted on bringing her to Hermione's villa?

She rose, picked up her evening bag, then saw a shadowy figure in a white dinner jacket approach the small table.

"So this is where you're hiding?" Mallory accused. His sudden appearance at the moment she was chafing at his apparent neglect caused her legs to tremble and she sank into the chair she had just vacated.

"I was just going to my room," she managed to gasp, for her throat felt dry.

"Then if you're tired, I mustn't keep you." His voice was cool and since she could not see the expression on his face, she was uncertain of his mood. She wanted to assure him that she would gladly sit up all night if she could sit with him and talk.

"No, no, I'm not really tired," she murmured. "I was – er – just enjoying sitting here." But that was a clumsy thing to say if he were quick enough to retort that he was sorry to disturb her.

Fortunately he said nothing, but sat opposite her and leaned his elbows on the table.

"Have you enjoyed this week-end?" he asked after a long pause.

"Very much indeed," she replied, wondering where this coolly polite exchange was intended to lead.

There was no time to wonder for long. A young footman, if that was his designation, came along the terrace, apologised for intruding and spoke to Mallory. Jacynth understood the gist of the message – that Mallory was wanted on the telephone, a call from New York, from Mr. Perandopoulos, Hermione's father.

With an "Excuse me" Mallory followed the young man and Jacynth was alone again. After a moment or two, she rose and walked the few steps towards a door leading into the villa, but before she reached there, Hermione came towards her in the glowing amber dress.

"Oh, Miss – er – I do apologise for not remembering your name – "

"Rowan. Jacynth Rowan," Jacynth answered stonily.

"Of course. I've been looking for you during the evening, but perhaps you found the society of my friends rather overwhelming."

"I'm not used to a wealthy environment, if that is your meaning."

"Exactly. And it must be very clear to you that you would not fit into Mallory's world."

"Was there any question of my fitting into Mr. Brendon's world?" Jacynth queried. "I'm his secretary, that's all."

"That's all?" echoed Hermione sarcastically. "But you'd give a great deal to be something more than that. Admit the truth."

"I consider that any ambitions I may have are my own concern." Jacynth did not intend to be bullied into any such admission.

Hermione laughed softly. "Your answer gives you away, but I must warn you that any favours Mallory shows you mean absolutely nothing. Where women are concerned, he is quite unyielding, although he's accustomed to many girls trying to break down his defences. That girl – your predecessor, I believe she was – she tried very hard, but of course she couldn't possibly succeed. In any case, she did not know that Mallory's affections are already engaged elsewhere."

"By 'elsewhere', you mean in your direction?" Jacynth queried.

"It must be obvious, I think, even to you, blinded as you

may be by believing that you're in love with him, that there is only one woman who really counts in his life."

"Yourself."

"Naturally. We have been friends for a long time and – I must speak plainly – I intend to marry him."

"Then what makes you suspect that you have anything to fear from me?" With a supreme effort Jacynth kept her voice steady and controlled.

"Oh, I'm not in the least concerned with any opposition from you. As it happens, I like you. In fact, I like you better than any of the other innumerable girls and women who have tried to force their way into Mallory's life. And it's because I admire you that I don't want to see you hurt. You're young and vulnerable, and it would be a pity if – "

"Thank you for your concern, Miss Perandopoulos," Jacynth interrupted, "but I think I'm quite capable of managing my own affairs."

"'Affairs' is an unfortunate word to use," Hermione said smoothly, "for these brief encounters leave no lasting impression on Mallory. They merely mean heartache for the girl."

Jacynth tried to make a move to leave her hostess, but Hermione stood resolutely in front of her. "If you'll take my advice, Miss – er – Rowland – you'll do your best to find a reason for returning to England as quickly as possible. Perhaps you have a relative who might be ill? Your mother? Or father?"

"My parents are dead and I couldn't rely on other members of my family to time their ill-health so accurately. But I'll bear your warning in mind and I do assure you that I have no wish to compete with you."

She felt Hermione's bristling anger. "You're extremely insolent. There's no question of competition."

"I apologise for my rudeness. I probably spoke too bluntly, but – "

She broke off as footsteps sounded close by and Mallory appeared.

Hermione turned swiftly towards him. "Your secretary and I have had a most friendly chat. Did you speak to my father on the telephone?"

"No. Something went haywire with the line and I couldn't make any kind of contact. He'll probably ring tomorrow if there's anything important."

So now Jacynth knew that the supposed telephone call was a fake, a ruse on Hermione's part to entice Mallory out of the way.

Now Hermione linked her arm in Mallory's and drew him away along the terrace. As soon as the way was clear, Jacynth went into the house and up to her room. For some time she relaxed in an armchair, pondering the events of the day, a day of which Mallory had spent a large part in her company. This morning's visit to the acropolis in Lindos, then this afternoon he had come down to the beach. She would not flatter herself by believing that he had actually come in search of her, but at least he had stayed with her a long time when he could have gone elsewhere.

His absence from the villa had obviously been noted by Hermione who had decided to lose no further time, but warn off a possible rival.

Jacynth laughed softly. A ludicrous situation! Did Hermione Perandopoulos, an exceedingly wealthy heiress, young and supremely beautiful, sincerely imagine that she was menaced by an insignificant secretary? It dawned on Jacynth that perhaps she should be flattered indeed that Hermione thought it necessary or advisable to give her a rap on the knuckles. A thrill of exultation ran through Jacynth, but she quickly suppressed it with cold reasoning. She must try to put this disturbing man out of her thoughts altogether. What had possessed her to fall in love with a man like Mallory? Was she so impressionable that she was over-ready to give her heart to any attractive man who came within her orbit? Vague memories of David came into her mind. She had believed herself completely heartbroken when Sara had disclosed her engagement to David, but now she, Jacynth, could dismiss that affection as a transient attraction. Certainly a separation of some couple of thousand miles had helped to dull the grief, if only to land her in yet another situation of the same kind.

But now her thoughts came up sharply against the realisation that the love she felt for Mallory could not be compared with any other emotion in her life. Perhaps it would be wise to adopt Hermione's suggestion and leave Mallory's employ and the island of Rhodes at the earliest opportunity.

Ironically, it occurred to her that she still did not know if he intended to keep her here or ship her back to England. That latter alternative might, indeed, prove a solution to her present misery.

On the way back to the Villa Kalakos next morning, Jacynth would really have preferred to sit in the back of the car instead of so close to Mallory in front. No amount of warning, advice or admonition from Hermione could suppress the throbbing excitement that Jacynth experienced with Mallory at her elbow. In vain she tried to calm herself, but in the end, yielded to the intoxication of the moment while it lasted.

At the Villa Kalakos a letter awaited her. Sara, her cousin, had written saying that she and David would be spending part of their honeymoon in Greece. "Would it be possible to come and see you?" Sara wrote. "I feel rather responsible about you and think I ought to make sure that you're working for a respectable man and living in comfortable conditions. If you'd rather not meet David just yet, I won't bring him along when we meet. I don't want you to be distressed, although probably by now you've got over some of your disappointment. We expect to be in Rhodes about the middle of May, so let me know where we can meet . . ."

Jacynth smiled as she read the letter. Dear, tactful Sara, who would leave her newly-acquired husband waiting in a café rather than inflict further unhappiness on a foolish girl who had extricated herself from one tangle only to fall headlong into another.

Sara would indeed laugh if Jacynth revealed the truth.

Would Mallory Brendon pass Sara's test of respectability? That query was unlikely to arise, for Jacynth had no right to invite her friends to the villa. She would have to meet Sara elsewhere.

Now that Mallory was back in his own house, Jacynth noticed a complete change from his relaxed, more casual and friendly attitude during the week-end at Lindos. He was cool and detached, gave her an enormous amount of work to do and was frequently out of the house for long periods. On these occasions he left no address or telephone number where he could be contacted and Jacynth was forced to answer enquirers with vague promises of ringing back when he was available.

One day a call came from Hermione Perandopoulos, who became irritated when Jacynth gave her the usual stock answer.

"Oh, please don't try to be so important," snapped Hermione. "Surely a good secretary knows where she can contact her employer? I have something urgent to discuss with him."

"I'm sorry, Miss Perandopoulos, but I assure you I really don't know where Mr. Brendon is or when he'll return here."

"Then what do you do if some urgent matter arises?" demanded Hermione.

"I have to say exactly what I'm saying now," returned Jacynth, careful to keep her voice smooth and polite. Then, in a genuine desire to assist Hermione, she added, "Perhaps you would know better than I where Mr. Brendon is likely to be spending his time."

But that innocent remark served only to increase Hermione's fury. "Naturally I know most of Mallory's friends," she asserted, "but I've been brought up by my father not to mix business and pleasure, so I don't wish to ring his friends."

"Then I'm sorry I can't help you any further," said Jacynth.

"I don't know whether you're being unhelpful, extremely rude or exceptionally discreet. Please tell Mr. Brendon that I called and ask him to ring me at the Summer Palace hotel."

"Certainly, Miss Perandopoulos, I'll do that."

Jacynth let out a great sigh as she put down the phone. A fantastic notion now occurred to her that Hermione perhaps suspected that Mallory was spending part of his time with another woman and she wanted to check up on him.

The notion made Jacynth smile. If that were the case, Hermione was showing signs of jealousy and that might indicate that either she loved Mallory or was anxious not to allow him to slip from her grasp.

Dutifully Jacynth wrote down on the desk-pad, "4.0 p.m. Miss Perandopoulos. Ring Summer Palace." When she went into Mallory's study next morning, the pad with its messages was exactly as she had left it. Either he had not returned home the previous night or he had ignored all his callers, including Hermione.

At lunch Jacynth made discreet enquiries of Caterina, who disclosed that the master had returned in the early hours of the morning and left again at six.

"Sometimes he spends evenings with friends and then he gets up early to go fishing," said Caterina.

Jacynth could not believe that she understood the Greek words. "Fishing? *Psvrema?*"

Caterina indicated agreement.

Jacynth asked no further questions, but when the housekeeper had cleared away, the girl laughed. "Fishing!" she muttered to herself. "A fine tale!" All the same, she wondered what Mallory Brendon was up to – if, that is, he was up to anything at all

Then one day a week or so later when business routine had settled into its more normal groove, he came into her office and demanded answers to a whole string of questions. At first she had assumed he was contrite about his aloofness and was trying to establish a more cordial atmosphere, but as he delved more and more into what she regarded as her own private life, she became puzzled and slightly irritated.

He had already asked about her parents and how long since they had died. "So you've been on your own for more than two years, since your mother died?"

"I shared a flat in London with a distant cousin." It occurred to her now that she might mention Sara's probable visit. "She's coming here soon – on her honeymoon – so perhaps she could call here one day?"

"By all means," he answered casually. Then he was back at his questioning, asking how she filled in her spare time. What were her chief interests? Dancing? Discothèques?

"Dancing, of course," she replied. "But I'm not fond of discos. I prefer concerts or theatres when possible and during last winter I went to French conversation classes."

He raised his eyebrows at that and gave her that slightly sardonic smile that had such a devastating effect on her.

"And now you're adding Greek to your linguistic abilities."

Jacynth was tempted to ask him how he enjoyed his early morning fishing and what other pursuits he might have, but she bit back the impulsive words, remembering that he was still her employer, with power to fire her or continue to hire her.

Then, after it seemed he had investigated her background and she had imagined it was because of his genuine interest in her, he exploded her rosy fancies with a laconic, "I shall need your passport tomorrow. I have to apply for a work-permit for you."

He went out of the room before she could recover her wits enough to say anything, either in gratitude because he evidently intended to keep her in Rhodes, or to verify that at last she had worked satisfactorily.

In fact, she hardly knew whether to be grateful or not for his decision. In a sense, she had been half hoping that he might send her home on the grounds of inefficiency. That would have been an ignominious dismissal, but perhaps easier to bear than the constant anguish of loving him in the knowledge that he would never return that affection, that he would never gaze at her with love in his eyes.

When she handed him her passport next day, she said tentatively, "So I'm to be allowed to stay a little longer?"

He was sitting at his desk in the study and now ran his fingers through his thick, dark hair in a gesture she had come to recognise as one he used when he wanted to avoid an immediate reply.

"It seems I have little choice. If I send you home, heaven knows what sort of substitute I might get as a replacement, and in the meantime, the work piles up."

"I'm sorry if I haven't given you much satisfaction," she said demurely.

His reaction was startling. "Satisfaction!" He roared the word at her. "What the blazes do you mean by that?"

Jacynth took a step backwards away from the desk. "Only that – that my work hasn't been always what you wanted, but I've done my best."

"Yes, you have done your best," he muttered savagely. "Done your best to ruin – " he broke off, as though only now aware that she was standing only a few feet away. "Leave me and get on with whatever job you're doing."

Thoroughly alarmed, she scuttled out of the room as fast as possible. In her office she stared at her typewriter. What did he mean? – "done your best to ruin – "? What had she ruined for him? Surely not even Hermione could accuse her of ruining the relationship between the Greek girl and Mallory.

On the other hand, it was Mallory who had ruined Jacynth's peace of mind. Never again, she thought – at least for a long time to come – would she know contentment. Perhaps her best course now would be to go back to his study and snatch away the passport which he needed for application for her work-permit. She had only to walk out of her office, along the corridor and into his study, but her body refused to act; she stood up and walked towards the door, but, knowing she was a coward, retraced her steps and sat down. Tears blurred the words of the document she was trying to copy and she brushed them away angrily.

There were times when she hated Mallory with every ounce of resentment she could muster. His cold moods, his brusque treatment of her even though she slaved all hours, his reluctance ever to praise or encourage her over the work. So what was left that was, in Diana's words, "irresistible?" Only physical attraction. That was the plain answer, and Jacynth reckoned that she ought to be old enough now to realise how little the magnet of masculine virility was worth unless it was accompanied by a good deal more. Understanding, respect, minds that could travel on the same wavelength – these were some of the essential qualities necessary for a happy marriage.

Suddenly she pulled herself together. What was she dreaming of, drivelling on like this about problematic marriages? From now on for the length of her stay in Rhodes she must steel herself to work like an automaton, impervious to her employer's taunts or moods and even more armoured against the rare smile or compliment that came her way.

When Mallory announced two days later that he was flying to Crete and would be away for at least four days, she heaved a sigh of relief, but suppressed it almost immediately. She was not quick enough, for he said, "Does that sigh indicate your pleasure in being rid of me?"

"It wasn't meant to," she replied.

"You're too transparent, Jacynth," he said, harshly, but she revelled in his use of her first name. "You might at least try to dissemble and pretend that the days will be over-long without me."

"I expect you'll leave me enough work to occupy me so that the days won't exactly drag," she retorted, unaware of the sharply acid tone she had used.

"That depends on how you arrange the work. With a little manipulation, you might even manage to take a day off and go shopping or sightseeing if you choose."

Forgetful of his advice not to display her feelings so openly, she relaxed into a delighted smile. "Thank you, Mr. Brendon."

"There you go again – all charm and eagerness to please," he muttered. Without another word, he turned swiftly and went back to his study.

Put my foot in it again, she thought resentfully. Why must he tread me down so forcibly whenever I find a grain of pleasure? She bent down to pick up some papers from the floor. "Yes, I'll be glad when he goes," she said aloud, "so that I can laugh when I like."

"How pleasant that you can find something to laugh at!" His voice startled her and she lifted her head so quickly that she bumped her forehead on the corner of the table.

"Not usually when you're here." The impulsive words rushed out before she could stop them. She stared up at him, appalled at her own spurt of ill-temper. Then, because his level glance disturbed her and caused her heart to hammer so loudly that she believed he must hear it, she plunged still deeper into a clash. "I wish you wouldn't spy on me," she began angrily. She refused to look at him and added, "Well, it makes me feel uncomfortable and – "

When she looked across at him, he was bowing to her with his hand on his heart. "Dear Miss Rowan – I'd better be quite formal – in future I'll knock very loudly on this door if I suspect that you're talking to yourself. I came back only to remind you of the schedule I'd like done first – if I may humbly mention it."

He was openly laughing at her, deriding her for her temerity, but she supposed she deserved it and was probably fortunate that he did not fly off the handle and flay her with his sarcastic tongue.

After Mallory had left for Crete, Jacynth worked hard the first day almost without a break so that on the second she could take some time off, as he had given her permission.

First, though, she explored the garden of the Villa Kalakos more thoroughly. By now Nikon had tidied the paths, planted flower beds and not only cleaned the swimming pool, but filled it. Later, she would swim there, although she preferred the sea, especially as an excellent beach was only a few yards from the villa, across the road and the promenade.

The windmill still intrigued her and she poked at the wooden door at the base, but it refused to budge. When she asked Nikon if it were possible to enter, he frowned and scowled and said it would be full of rats and mice.

"What does it look like inside?" she wanted to know.

He shrugged his thick shoulders, then pushed the door open. "Wait!" he commanded. But no small creatures emerged and he allowed her to peer inside the stone tower. At first she could see nothing but vague darkness, but as her eyes grew accustomed to the dimness, she made out the shape of a millstone and remnants of machinery. An old ladder with broken rungs leaned against the wall.

Her curiosity satisfied, Jacynth stepped out of the tower and allowed Nikon to pull the door into position.

"A pity to let it go to ruin," she commented, but the man merely smiled.

"No use any more," he muttered.

Jacynth disagreed, but she was not in a position to argue with him. In England she had read of windmills turned into handsome and individually styled dwellings. But apparently here in Rhodes, there were so many disused windmills that they had lost their novelty and no one wanted to use them.

Each morning Mallory telephoned from Crete asking what had arrived in the post and Jacynth was appreciative of the trust he placed in her that he allowed her to open all his letters, except those that were obviously marked "Private".

She gave him a resumé of the work she had completed and told him when she had taken time off. On the day, however, when she had intended to put in a full eight hours' stint, a telephone call from Ray Gurney urged her to drop everything and come out with him for most of the day.

"I've hired a car here on the island," he told her, "and we can go where we like. I have to visit a particular pottery, but you'd have no objection to that, would you?"

"I'm not sure how to answer," she temporised. "I'd no idea you were back from England."

"Yes, I'm launching out now. I've fixed up a temporary office in Athens and I'm staying in Rhodes for a few days. I can't afford hotels, now that I have to pay my own expenses, so I've taken a room over a shop in the Old City. Now what time will you be ready?"

"I don't think I could manage today."

"Why not? Is that old tyrant going to stop you?"

"He isn't – " Jacynth began, then realised that if she disclosed Mallory's absence, she would hand Ray all the best reasons for persuading her to play truant. "Look," she said quickly, "let me work this morning and I could meet you after lunch. How about that?"

"Not much good," he said flatly. "All the people I want to visit will be taking their siesta."

"What about tomorrow?" she suggseted.

"No, it's got to be today – or not at all," he said abruptly. "Perhaps you don't really *want* to come."

"It isn't that," she assured him. "The point is that I didn't plan to take time off today and I don't see how I can – "

"Oh, I bet if that old Greek boss of yours asked you out for a day, you wouldn't hesitate. You'd drop everything and jump into his car."

She laughed softly to hide her embarrassment. Ray was certainly correct. "Well, the situation isn't quite the same, is it? If Mr. Brendon wanted me to go out – which is quite unlikely – we should be together and there would be no question of my taking time off unknown."

"Well, ask him now. Tell him – "

"I can't," she interrupted. "He's out for the day." That at least was true. Then she saw that it might be more advantageous to accept Ray's invitation for today while Mallory was away than for Ray to cajole her at a time when her employer was present.

"All right," she said. "Give me half an hour and I'll be ready, but I must come back early in the evening and finish the work I'm doing."

"Oh, you do make a martyr of yourself over that man's work," he burst out angrily. "All right, I suppose I'll have to be satisfied with the few crumbs you can spare." He cut off abruptly, leaving her with the feeling that she regretted now not refusing altogether. She tidied the papers on her desk, locked away the confidential files in Mallory's study and went to the kitchen to tell Caterina that she would be out most of the day, but home in the evening.

"Don't cook anything for me for dinner," she said. Then she noticed how ill Caterina seemed. The woman was sitting at the table, her shoulders bent and her thin face drawn.

"Are you ill, Caterina?" Jacynth asked.

"No." She added that she was only resting and would take it easy during the day.

As she went to her room and changed her dress, Jacynth reflected that Caterina seemed to have an enormous amount of housework and cooking to do. Even if some of the rooms in the Villa were not used much, the others had to be kept clean and there were two main meals to cook every day. Undoubtedly Nikon helped with some of the heavier tasks and probably cleaned the fearsome-looking stove in the kitchen, but Caterina was still fully occupied day after day.

Jacynth picked up her wide-brimmed straw hat and went outside to wait for Ray. He came along the street almost immediately and she admired the dashing maroon car he had hired.

"I'd a good mind not to bother with you at all," he said by way of greeting. "So reluctant to enjoy a day's pleasure."

She laughed, as she settled herself in the car. "If I'd known earlier, I might have arranged the time off better, but your call was out of the blue."

"All the more reason you ought to have been thrilled about it," he returned smugly.

"Well, tell me about your business affairs," she suggested, attempting to turn his attention away from herself and what he imagined should be her reaction.

"Oh, rattling along quite well so far. I came to Athens nearly a week ago and I've made good contacts with quite a number of promising firms."

"And how did you get on with your company in England?"

Ray grinned and then let out a sharp explosion of derisive amusement. "Oh, they made a bit of a song and dance about my leaving. They said I was poaching on their ground if I was setting up in Greece, but they couldn't do anything about it. They could hardly expect me to set up shop in the Arctic Circle, could they?"

"I suppose they thought you were using knowledge you'd gained by working for them and putting it to your own interests."

"Exactly. And who would blame me for that?"

Jacynth remained silent for a few moments. While there was probably nothing completely dishonest in Ray's working outlook, she thought privately that his principles were those of a cut-throat go-getter. He thought nothing of "ditching", as he termed it, the firm which had given him his first chance of acting as purchasing agent abroad. More than that, she guessed he would use the information acquired on their behalf and shape it to further his own ends.

"I've one substantial advantage," he continued, after a pause. "I know all the customers my old firm supplied and while I keep my overheads low, I can undercut their prices. I'm pretty sure I can drive hard bargains at this end, even though Greeks are pretty tough in that respect."

"Isn't that rather unscrupulous?" she queried mildly. "To use your firm's customers in England, I mean."

"Good heavens, no! That's business. What about your precious boss? Do you think he stops to consider someone's personal feelings when he's out to make a deal?"

"No, I hadn't thought of it like that," she admitted. Perhaps the fact that Mallory's business dealings were on the grand scale, compared to Ray's trivial transactions, removed them to the world of high finance, but the principles of fairness should still apply. Now she wondered if her emotional involvement with Mallory had blinded her to a similar lack of scruples.

But Ray was already launching into an account of an interview in Athens with a supplier of metalwork belts and necklaces. Jacynth listened with only half her attention, for now he was driving through the outskirts of Rhodes town and skirting the hill called Monte Smith, named, so she had discovered, after a British admiral who lived there in Napoleon's time.

"It's an odd name," she said. "Sounds like a pop singer."

"What does?" he demanded.

"The hill. Monte Smith."

"Oh, that. Well, as I was telling you – " Ray was off again, although Jacynth would have liked him to stop nearby so that she could see the ancient stadium and the ruins of a theatre and the temple of Apollo. But she knew it was no use expecting Ray to pander to her wish for sightseeing when he was anxious to reach his destination as fast as possible.

She had gauged the approximate distance from the Villa Kalakos and one day when she had the leisure she would take a taxi and explore the site.

"You won't mind if I leave you to wander around the showroom while I talk to the man I want to see?" queried Ray, when they arrived at the pottery.

"Not at all. I shall be quite happy roaming around."

She saw at once, although she had no expert knowledge of ceramics, that the products turned out here were far superior in style and finish than some of those in the souvenir shops. Better, too, than the quality of the two small Greek vases Ray had given her, one of which had shattered into dust when Mallory knocked it.

There were trays and bowls, mounted tiles to hang as pictures or use as small cocktail mats, all with engaging designs of ships or donkeys, flowers or birds, in vivid colours that avoided being garish.

Such variety made it difficult to decide which to purchase, but eventually Jacynth chose a fairly lightweight tray for Sara and a couple of wall pictures for herself, one displaying a galleon with billowing sails and the traditional eye painted on the bows, the other an ornately-feathered duck with a fish in its beak.

When Ray rejoined her, he seemed elated at his business success. He was almost rubbing his hands with glee when he explained the low prices he had been able to agree on with the owner. As he took her wrapped purchases to stow in the car, he frowned. "You paid ordinary retail prices for this stuff?" he asked.

"Of course," Jacynth agreed.

"That was stupid of you. I could easily have worked a discount for you. How much did they cost?"

Jacynth reddened. "Trivial amounts. One tray and two small pictures. They were quite inexpensive and I wouldn't have expected any discount."

Ray sniffed with displeasure. "Then in future, don't be so ready to part with your money if I'm around. I can get a bit knocked off almost anything here in Rhodes."

Jacynth entered the car and said nothing. Even a substantial discount would have made little difference to the prices she had paid and Ray's intensely commercial attitude annoyed her.

He took her to lunch at a roadside café where the proprietor, who looked more like a bandit living in the hills, thought Jacynth, than a café owner, served an excellent meal of *plaki*, a fish dish with oil, tomatoes and herbs, followed by the spicy minced beef balls called *keftedes*, to which she was now quite accustomed.

"Stephanos, the boss, makes some very good pastry filled with hot cheese," Ray told her. "Care to try some?"

"If I can manage it," she answered with a grin, feeling her waistline. "Soon I shall have no waist at all, only a barrel shape."

Ray laughed, reached across and placed his hand along her ribs, giving her a gentle squeeze. "Not too much padding yet," he observed.

When the little flaky-pastry triangles filled with cheese arrived and Jacynth saw they were quite small, her attention was divided between the food which was delicious and the lack of sensation when Ray had hugged her waist. If Mallory had touched her in even a featherweight gesture, her reaction would have been quite different – her pulses leaping, a delicious excitement coursing her veins. But with Ray there was no such effect and she decided, ruefully, that perhaps it was just as well that both men did not agitate her in a similar fashion.

Later in the afternoon Ray drove down towards the coast where there was a small deserted beach of coarse shingle.

"Brought your swimsuit?" he asked.

"Well, no, I didn't think we'd be near a beach – or that you'd have time for anything so frivolous as bathing," she added with a smile.

"Why not? I've always time – or, at least generally, for beach games with a pretty girl. You don't need me to tell you that your looks are quite stunning."

"Thank you," she said demurely, although she was aware that Ray had an eye for most girls who were not cross-eyed or possessed hare-lips, and owned reasonable figures.

"I always bring swimming trunks with me in a car, just in case there's a chance for a swim, although if there's no one about I don't always bother, just go in nude. Much more pleasurable."

When she made no response, he grasped her arm persuasively. "Come on, don't be shy. I'll turn my back until you're in the water. Lots of girls do without their bikinis."

"I'm not one of them."

"But there isn't a soul about," he protested.

"Anyone might come down here suddenly – and besides, it's daylight." But that was a mistake, as she immediately discovered.

"Ha! So you wouldn't mind in the dark – or moonlight!"

"No, I didn't say that at all. You go and swim if you want to. I'm not stopping you."

Ray flung away from her. "You're the most prudish thing since 1860!" He lit a cigarette, half smoked it, then threw it away. "All right, I'll go in alone. You're not much of a girl for a bit of fun, are you?"

"No, perhaps not," she agreed stonily. "It depends on what sort of fun."

He went back to the car and emerged a few minutes later wearing dark blue trunks. He sat beside her, then lay back full length, his hands behind his head. She had tilted her large straw hat over her face and was unprepared when his arm suddenly shot out and grasped her shoulder. She was imprisoned, held firmly down on the shingly beach, then the pressure of his mouth on her lips caused her a feeling of panic, but as she struggled to move her face away, he tightened his grip.

"Please, Ray – let me go – " she managed to whisper when he raised her to a half-sitting position in his arms. She could feel his fingers fumbling with the zip at the back of her dress and she took advantage of that slight relaxing of his hold to wrench herself away. But now he pulled the dress off her shoulder, pressed fierce kisses on her flesh and forced her back again on the uncomfortable beach.

Jacynth was aware of the hard strength of his body and his urge to conquer her and she recoiled from surrender. She managed to free one hand and, doubling her fist, pushed his mouth away from her cheek.

"You're hurting me!" she cried out, as the sharp edges of shingle dug into her back. He sat up and moved away from her as suddenly as he had first embraced her.

"No, you're not much fun," he muttered morosely.

She was too choked to answer, for panic still enveloped her like an evil cloud. She was alone with Ray on a completely deserted beach with no habitation nearer than several miles and her only means of transport, apart from her own feet, the car. If she tried to run for safety, he would overtake her in a matter of minutes, for the ground at the top of the beach was rough and stony with tussocks of grass. Her best plan, she thought, was to try to calm him down. Yet if she showed him the intense coldness she felt, that might be further provocation.

To her relief, he rose now and ambled off towards the sea. When he came out of the water she was sitting in the shade of the car. He towelled himself and occasionally glared at her. Droplets of water clung to his chest and shoulders and instantly she recalled that day in Lindos when Mallory had helped to dry her back and she had tingled with delight at his touch.

This man, Ray Gurney, evoked no response in her at the sight of his athletic figure, the fair smooth skin and the tufts of down on his chest. She could only try to put Mallory in his place, but that was entirely futile.

"I wonder if you'd shout for help if you were down here alone with that boss of yours," Ray muttered as he pulled his shirt over his head.

When she did not answer, he seized her wrist. "Well! Why don't you answer?"

"The situation wouldn't arise," Jacynth said more coolly than she felt.

"But how you hope it would!" he jeered. "You've gone overboard for him, I really do believe, but how far will that get you?"

"If I had gone overboard for him, it wouldn't get me anywhere."

"I'm glad you realise that. He'd never marry you, no matter what happened. I don't suppose you're the first pretty secretary he's had – and sent packing when he was tired of her."

"Mr. Brendon is probably going to marry a very wealthy Greek heiress," Jacynth said emphatically, trying to stop this conversation heading for even more dangerous channels.

"Oh, indeed! Nothing like money attracting money."

"Probably at some time in the future you yourself might be glad to find a girl with some financial backing," she snapped.

To her surprise, he smiled. "I suppose I deserved that. I guess you're about right. Girls with money – or well-to-do fathers – aren't exactly growing on trees, but I'd be prepared to take on someone with brains as well as looks. That's why I like you, Jacynth." He bent down and took her hand gently in his. "Together we could do great things. I couldn't afford to marry yet – but – "

"I like you, too, Ray," she interrupted, forcing warmth into her tone. "So don't let's spoil everything by your being too impulsive."

He puffed out a sigh of resignation, and gave her a defeated kind of smile.

"All right. We'll keep it all on a business footing – for the time being. Don't forget that soon I'll be able to give you at least as good a job as you have now – probably better. More interesting, anyway. In due course, we might even go into partnership – in every way."

She smiled at him, appreciative of his ability to control himself and switch his mind to his commercial ambitions. "I'll remember what you say. Now, could we go home soon? I still have a lot of work to do tonight."

"Huh! Work for that man is all you think about."

"You'll be the same when your business is flourishing," she reminded him. "Some of your social dates will have to be abandoned if you have an important deal coming up or have to sit somewhere and work out a list of prices."

Now he laughed. "You hit the target fair and square, don't you? All right, there'll be no more pleasure in the day, so we might as well go home. Actually, I could do with an hour or so tonight myself, working on some invoices."

Even so, Jacynth arrived at the Villa Kalakos later than she had intended and prevailed on Ray to drop her outside the gates. Nikon opened the door to her and, with a murmured greeting, she hurried past him and fled swiftly up the stairs, but she had gained less than half a dozen before a voice compelled her to turn. Mallory stood at the foot of the staircase, his face stern and his eyes cold.

"So you've been out most of the day?" he queried.

"Yes, but I intend to do some of the work now."

"You'd better come in here and we'll discuss what needs to be done."

He waited while she reluctantly descended the stairs and joined him in the office sitting room.

"I have been out most of today," she said, "but I think you'll find I've not slacked on the important matters."

He was staring at her, his dark eyes glittering with an expression she could not fathom.

"With that boy-friend of yours?"

"Yes."

"He's apparently acquired a car to take you about."

"He has hired one here in Rhodes."

"Turn round," he commanded. She had been most careful not to display her back view with the top of her dress ripped and the zip useless. In the car she had done her best to fasten the dress with a safety pin, and unfortunately, today of all days, she had not taken with her any kind of jacket or scarf to hide the damage.

"Turn round, I said." His voice was even harsher than usual and she knew that if she hesitated any longer to obey, he would forcibly seize her shoulders and twist her.

"An accident with your dress?" he asked sardonically.

"Yes. The zip caught and – and I – tore it – we were going swimming – "

His contemptuous smile chilled her heart. "I see. And I suppose your impatient fingers did this damage to the rest of your back. Or was it someone else's hands clawing at you?"

"The beach was – rather stony," she muttered.

He came behind her and unfastened the safety pin, while Jacynth stood there trembling with mingled terror and ecstasy. Was he going to repeat that incident of a few weeks ago when he had savagely kissed her after Ray had left?

Now he inspected the scratches and bruises on her back, then twisted her to face him, pulling down the shoulder of her dress. Abruptly, he jerked the dress up again to her neck.

"You need have no fears from me," he assured her, and she heard the whiplash of scorn in his words. "I'm not aching to kiss you where other men have planted their lips. You'd better put some ointment on those grazes and scratches."

"But when I've changed my dress, I'll come down and – "

"You'll do nothing of the kind. Just go. The work can wait."

In her room she felt as though she had been publicly whipped. Of course he had seen her back as she ascended the stairs immediately after she had entered the front door. Returning earlier than he had said he would from Crete and then spying on her. Waiting for her, ready to pounce.

But her resentment and indignation gave way to tears of grief that he believed that she had allowed Ray to make love to her, when there was only one man in the world to whom she would so gladly make the sweet surrender.

CHAPTER SEVEN

AFTER Jacynth had showered, dabbed cream on her back and dressed again, she wondered if Mallory intended to send her supperless to bed, the conventional punishment for naughty children. But she saw no reason to skulk in her room and marched resolutely downstairs, hoping that Mallory was not in her office.

There were no signs of a meal being laid and she went to the kitchen, where Nikon was stirring something in a saucepan. She guessed immediately that Caterina was definitely ill, and Nikon confirmed, half in English, half in Greek, that his wife had severe pains and had gone to bed.

"But the doctor?" queried Jacynth.

"No, not yet." He added that Caterina would probably recover by the morning, but Jacynth was alarmed and asked if she could go up and see Caterina.

The housekeeper lay with eyes closed when the girl entered the room, but at the sound of Nikon's voice, she turned over and smiled at Jacynth, apologising for her inability to cook the evening dinner.

Jacynth waved away such apologies and asked if Mr. Brendon knew.

Nikon explained that he had told his master, who decided to go out for a meal.

"Tomorrow morning Caterina must have the doctor," Jacynth declared.

The woman answered weakly that tomorrow she would be better and not need the doctor.

Downstairs again, Jacynth arranged to share whatever meal Nikon was preparing for himself and as he had a pot of soup on the stove, she took up a portion to Caterina.

As she shared the smoked ham and salad, then some cheese,

with Nikon in the kitchen, he spoke of several other slight illnesses Caterina had suffered in the past year.

Now he shrugged his burly shoulders and told Jacynth that there was no need to worry. Caterina would recover quickly as she had in the past.

Jacynth promised to get up early next day and prepare her own coffee and rolls for breakfast. When she went into the kitchen just before half-past six next morning, she was surprised to find Mallory already there. He and Nikon were talking in Greek and Jacynth caught the gist of the conversation.

"How is Caterina?" asked Jacynth of Nikon, ignoring Mallory.

Mallory answered, "Not at her best, I'm afraid."

"She needs a doctor."

"We shall see later if that's necessary."

Indignation rose in Jacynth's throat like a gigantic marble. "How can you be so callous!" she demanded. "Caterina seemed desperately ill last night when I saw her."

Mallory gave her an oblique glance, arrogant and contemptuous. "Your coffee is ready. Perhaps you'll take your own tray and carry it somewhere. We're rather short-staffed here at present."

"I'll eat my breakfast here in the kitchen," she said defiantly, and sat down at the scrubbed table.

"As you wish," Mallory inclined his head almost graciously, then sat opposite her. This action disconcerted her, for she was acutely aware of his proximity, as always. He was wearing a dark blue brocade dressing-gown and his thick dark hair had not been disciplined into its normal tidiness.

After a moment or two Nikon left the kitchen to take some coffee to his wife.

"You must have realised," began Jacynth, losing no time in her attack, "that Caterina has far too much to do to run this house and cook all the meals. It's hardly to be wondered that occasionally she might crack up."

Mallory raised his eyebrows in a questioning glance.

"Are you now taking it upon yourself to run my house for me?"

She coloured furiously. "Not at all, but you could surely arrange for the housekeeper to have assistance."

"I've offered any amount of assistance – women to clean the house, girls to help with the cooking – but Caterina is stubborn – as you would understand if you knew anything about the Greek race."

She was temporarily silenced and gave her attention to her breakfast.

After a long pause, Mallory spoke again. "I understand that you've been in the habit for some time of cleaning and tidying your own bedroom."

"Is that an accusation?" she asked sharply. "I've been brought up not to leave my room looking as though an avalanche had hit it, and I thought I could save Caterina a small amount of extra work by making my own bed."

Mallory carefully buttered a piece of roll. Then he asked, "Do you know how to cook?"

Her mouth fell open in surprise. He was adept at avoiding a direct challenge, but flinging one back in return. "I can cook simple meals – after a fashion. Why?"

"Perhaps you could try your hand at simple meals for a day or two. Nikon is useful in many ways, but not exactly as a chef."

"I couldn't undertake to cook in the Greek manner."

"No one is asking you to do that. Merely to save us from starvation."

In spite of her angry determination not to yield meekly to his demands, Jacynth laughed. "Starvation?" she echoed. "There are restaurants not far away."

"Caterina's feelings would be hurt if she found out that we went out to our food. There's also Nikon to be thought of."

Jacynth was lost in trying to equate this strange man's sense of compassion with his relentless tyranny in other directions.

"I shall certainly need help from Nikon if I'm to use that frightful stove," she said at last.

"Naturally you've been accustomed to the luxury of electric or gas cookers," he gibed.

"I can't be expected to be in two places at once, slaving over a hot stove and – "

"Slaving over a typewriter," he finished for her. "Perhaps we can arrange short sessions for each of your activities."

She gently shook her head from side to side and smiled. "I see I can't win," she murmured.

"Of course it's no part of your contract as my secretary that you should help in the kitchen and you have every right to refuse."

"What would happen if I did refuse?" She was surprised at her own temerity in asking the question.

"I'll decide what course to take if and when that happens." He rose from the table, took his plate and cup and saucer to the sink. "The doctor will be here soon after nine o'clock. You'd better be around to take his instructions."

He went out of the kitchen before she could frame any reply. So he had already called the doctor?

When Nikon returned, Jacynth discussed what could be arranged and he agreed to help her wherever possible, although he pointed out that while he could make good coffee and tasty soup, this was the limit of his culinary talent.

Jacynth decided she could probably conjure up a moussaka for lunch if Nikon could prepare some of the ingredients. Fruit and cheese would have to complete the meal and Mallory would have to like it or lump it, she decided.

When she returned to her office sitting-room, she found a flat parcel on her table. She opened it to discover a handsome tile plaque of the Prince of the Lilies. There was nothing to indicate the sender, but only Mallory could have placed the gift there. A surge of great delight ran through her because he had not only brought her this token from Crete, but it represented an apology for breaking her Prince of the Lilies vase that Ray had given her.

She was still holding the plaque in her hands when Mallory came in.

"I thought you'd better have it now," he said, with a grin. "Otherwise you won't know if it's meant to be an award for your excellent cooking."

"You'd better wait and see what my cooking is like, but in the meantime, many thanks for the Prince. It's incomparable." She wanted to fling her arms around his neck and kiss him in the manner of a child who has been given a delightful present, but she restrained herself.

When the doctor came to see Caterina, he immediately ordered her to hospital.

"How serious?" asked Jacynth.

"Perhaps not very serious, but she must be examined properly and needs rest. I think she will not rest if she remains at home."

Jacynth agreed that Caterina would insist on getting up the moment she felt slightly better.

Mallory drove Caterina accompanied by her husband to the hospital, but Jacynth, who had offered to go as well, stayed at home to press on with her own work and then to attend to the cooking.

When Nikon returned alone in a taxi he was looking more cheerful. "Only a few days," he told Jacynth, "and she will be home again."

Jacynth hoped that would be true, not merely for her own sake, but for Nikon's.

Mallory did not come in for lunch but telephoned in the afternoon that he would be home about seven for dinner. "I can't wait to sample your delicacies," he said, and rang off before Jacynth could think of a suitable reply.

Nikon offered to go into the town and buy fresh red mullet, a supply of meat and fruit and vegetables which he did not grow himself.

Jacynth asked how often he had to shop in the usual way and he replied, "Every two days."

"Can't food and the rest be delivered?"

Nikon's face assumed a horrified expression. "Not fresh," he declared, and rambled on in his mixture of Greek and English that good food must be personally selected or else the suppliers would send you inferior stuff which they could not easily sell.

Jacynth agreed that this was no doubt the ideal way, in fact, the old traditional way, and obviously superior, as far as quality went, to stacking quantities into refrigerators.

When Nikon returned and laid out his purchases on the kitchen table, Jacynth's heart sank. Red mullet she had seen before in the raw state, but now there were cuts of meat of strange shapes and textures together with outsize onions, cabbages with crinkled leaves, aubergines and artichokes; one parcel contained small squids, *kalamarakia*, a dish which she had eaten but never before prepared, and on the edge of the table a large crayfish.

She instructed Nikon to put away some of the food into the refrigerator, but he took the squids outside and put them in a bucket of water.

She decided that she would start cooking at six o'clock and went back to her office to finish some typing. It then occurred to her that Mallory's bedroom had probably not been attended to and she went in search of Nikon to ask which room.

When he told her that he had himself made the bed and tidied the room, Jacynth hardly knew whether to be glad or sorry. Relieved in one sense that Mallory would not return home to an untidy room with an unmade bed, she yet longed for a glimpse of his room, so that she could visualise him when he occupied it.

She pushed these futile thoughts out of her mind and concentrated on the work in hand, conscious that having spent most of the previous day with Ray, she was already far behind schedule.

When later she joined Nikon in the kitchen, she found him very useful. He prepared the fish, peeled and chopped onions and showed her which saucepans and frying pans to use.

Mallory came into the kitchen when she was putting the finishing touches to a dish that purported to be *keftedes*, spiced meat-balls, but some of them would not keep their rounded shape and fell apart.

"Too much meat, not enough bread," was Mallory's verdict.

"I have the fish course ready," she told him. "I'll serve it in five minutes if you'll go into the dining room."

"Oh, dismissed, I see. Perhaps I'd better have an omelette after all."

"After all!" she echoed angrily. "After I've taken some trouble to please you with your own style of cooking!"

She raised her head to find his eyes glittering with amusement and her hands trembled. Oh, why did he have to come butting in just when she needed all her self-control to cope with such unexpected duties in his house?

When she went into the dining room to serve the red mullet she was only too conscious of his nearness. Surely he must hear her heart hammering so loudly that she seemed to have no other sound in her own ears.

"You must join me," he invited, pointing to a place on the opposite side of the table.

"I can't leave Nikon to eat alone," she objected, although she was eager to accept.

"Why not? Is he more important than I that he must have company?"

"Well, he's used to Caterina being there and – "

"And I'm used to eating alone."

In another moment he would retract his offer, and sacrificing herself to Nikon would bring her no reward. "All right," she said hastily, "I'll bring in the next course and join you, if I may."

Nikon had no objection to being left alone in the kitchen and Jacynth savoured the delight of sharing with her employer a meal she had cooked. It was the first time she had eaten in the dining room, for she had not visited it again after that early tour of inspection with Caterina. The room, in spite of its elegant furnishings, lacked the warmth of companionship. She could imagine a dozen people seated around the oval table, hear their animated conversation, see the glances, amused, surprised or displeased, that passed between them. But that was only in the mind. In actual fact she found it difficult to converse with Mallory during the meal, for she was acutely aware that only the present crisis of Caterina's illness had saved her from being in disgrace over last night's incident when she had returned so dishevelled after the outing with Ray.

Mallory was not very talkative either, and she had the impression that he now regarded as a mistake having invited her to eat at his table.

"I've some work to do later," he said when she brought in the coffee, "so you can bring me the brandy to my study. But there's no need for you to go on working. You've had a pretty full day and probably we'll catch up tomorrow."

She accepted her dismissal and retired to the kitchen to clear away and wash the dishes.

During the next three or four days Jacynth managed the double routine of typing Mallory's work and attending to the meals. Mallory was not liberal with his compliments and the nearest he came to a word of praise was when she served fried mussels followed by *pastitsio*, a concoction of macaroni, minced meat and browned béchamel sauce.

"Very good flavour," he pronounced, "but one of these days you must treat me to some of your own English dishes. Apple pie, for instance."

She smiled with pleasure and made a mental note to ask Nikon to obtain some apples.

"Nikon tells me he has found a young girl who could help with the housework," Mallory continued. "Probably you can find time to show her around the house when she comes tomorrow."

"Certainly. I'll do that."

Since the first evening when Mallory had invited Jacynth to join him in the dining room, he had not repeated the offer and, in a way, she was relieved to eat with Nikon in the kitchen, although when she served a meal to Mallory, she was always conscious of his devastating masculinity. Once, when she accidentally touched his shoulder, she almost dropped the dish of carrots in her hand, for her arm felt as if it were on fire.

When next day she took the girl whom Nikon introduced as Chloe to start on the upstairs rooms, Jacynth was full of curiosity to learn what Mallory's room looked like. The décor was more feminine than she had visualised, cream and turquoise walls, cream brocade curtains at the windows and a large double bed with an ornate bedhead wrought in brass.

A bedside table was piled with books and papers, as one would expect, but there was also a photograph in a silver frame, a portrait of a very beautiful woman with dark hair and gentle eyes. His mother?

Jacynth pulled herself together and gave the girl Chloe instructions, although her Greek was inadequate for the purpose and she resorted to pantomime gestures for sweeping and dusting.

Two mornings later, when Jacynth considered she had more or less mastered the new routine of the household, she rose very early, donned her bikini and an enveloping towelling wrap and went down to the seashore to bathe. Her favourite little strip of beach was close to a portion used by one of the hotels farther along the shore and two men were already setting out cushioned lounge chairs and umbrellas ready for the crowd of sunbathers who would settle themselves there in a couple of hours' time. After swimming around for a while, she turned on to her back and studied the aquamarine sky above her. Far off she could hear the sound of a motor-boat – the inevitable water-skier, she guessed. When she raised her head and glanced towards that direction, she recognised the unmistakable figure of Mallory, a golden-tanned body in black trunks skimming along the water in undulating loops as the boat swerved and turned.

She raised one arm to wave to him, but could not be sure that he had seen her, and now she noticed a second boat with its attendant skier approaching from the opposite direction.

The two boats seemed intent on a collision course and

Jacynth watched, fascinated, as the two skiers evaded each other. Then suddenly, to her horror, she saw that one of the boats was coming straight towards her at terrific speed. She struck out blindly in what she thought was the opposite direction, but something landed a paralysing blow on one side of her head and shoulder and the darkness overtook her.

When she opened her eyes, she blinked in puzzlement. A man's face was bending over her as she lay on some hard surface and when the mist cleared she saw that the face belonged to Mallory.

"Are you all right?" he asked.

"I – I think so." So she had not drowned after all, unless this was heaven and Mallory only a vision. "What happened?"

"That clumsy fool in the other boat made a sharp turn and the stern hit you and sent you under."

"But somebody fished me out?"

Mallory grinned and nodded. "I had that honour – and you were slippery as an eel."

The motor boat grounded on the beach and Mallory sprang out. Jacynth raised herself to a sitting position, but the pain in her shoulder twisted her face in anguish.

"Wait!" Mallory commanded, then bent forward and scooped her out of the boat as though she had been a large fish, but she was much more excited than the fish would have been. She longed for the brief moment to continue as he held her close to his chest, then set her down gently on the sand.

"Can you walk?" he asked.

"Oh yes," she affirmed, but her first steps were tottery. "I had a bathing wrap and sandals farther along." The boatman trotted along and retrieved the wrap, which Mallory then held and draped around her shoulders. Jacynth closed her eyes, partly because her shoulder ached and her head throbbed, but mainly because she was aware of his tender touch, the touch that aroused all her longing for the full embrace that might have followed.

In the next few moments he had pulled on his own towelling

wrap and thrust his feet into the sandals handed to him by the boatman.

"We'd better get home as quickly as possible," Mallory muttered, and took her arm to help her up the beach and across the road, completely ignorant of the intoxicated, heady sensation for which he was responsible.

He carried her up the stairs and into her room and she was nearly fainting with exultation. As he laid her on her bed and loomed over her, a tanned figure in a dark blue wrap, she became afraid to meet his eyes for fear of what he might see there.

"A pity this should happen when Caterina is away," he said.

"Oh, I shall be all right in half an hour," she assured him.

"You're probably still rather shocked. Take it easy for to-day. By the way, what made you come out for a swim so early? Or is it a habit?"

"No, this morning was the first time. I thought I could take the time then. Chloe, the girl recommended by Nikon, will do the housework, so I have only a bit of cooking to do, apart from your various documents."

Mallory's mouth relaxed into a smile. "You seem terrified of slacking. Do I really keep you in chains?"

"There are times when I feel that I'm not working hard enough," Jacynth admitted.

"That was only at first. I had to see what sort of stuff you were made of." He thrust his hands into the pockets of his wrap. "I'll telephone for the doctor to come and examine you later in the day. I think only bruises and a certain amount of shock, but we'd better make sure. We don't want a household minus both you and Caterina."

He leaned over her and she imagined for a wild instant that he was going to kiss her, but evidently he changed his mind, straightened up and stalked out of the room.

Her spirits, which had been so high during the last half-hour, slowly sank to zero. No, of course, he could not do without both herself and Caterina. That would be a disaster for both the smooth running of his business concerns and his household. How foolish of her to fancy that his consideration was on her own behalf as a person. He had rescued her when one of the boats hit her, but he was really rescuing his secretary and temporary cook, not Jacynth Rowan. Yet she regretted that she had not known that exquisite moment when he must have lifted her into the boat.

Chloe brought Jacynth's breakfast and Jacynth was grateful for the hot coffee. After a short rest she roused herself to shower and dress. Her shoulder was painful, but no bruise showed yet.

In the kitchen Nikon had already begun to prepare vegetables and expressed his concern about Jacynth's accident, adding that early morning skiers were a dangerous breed and motor-boats a menace.

She gave Chloe instructions about cleaning the various rooms and assured Nikon that there was no cause for alarm. Mallory had evidently announced that he would be out all day, so that meant that lunch need not be very elaborate and she could later on concentrate on the evening meal.

Typing was a different matter and her speed was slowed down considerably, but she doggedly stuck to the tasks awaiting her attention.

In the late afternoon the doctor came, and Jacynth was relieved to hear that apparently no bones were broken. The shoulder would ache for several days and probably bruising would appear. The side of her head was grazed just above the ear, and the doctor attended to this. In excellent English he instructed her to come to his surgery if any further treatment should be needed, or if she became worried about her injuries.

When Mallory returned in the early evening she asked at what time he would like his dinner served.

His glance was directed at some papers on his desk and he did not look up. "Oh, just bring me something on a tray – an omelette – anything – and a glass of wine."

"But I've made you an apple pie!" she protested.

"Apple pie?" His puzzled glance indicated that he had never heard of such a strange dish.

"Yes, you suggested it as an English sweet."

His face cleared and he half smiled. "Oh, yes, so I did. I wonder if that was wise. All right, bring in whatever you've concocted."

Fine thanks I get for pandering to his lordship's whims! Jacynth thought rebelliously as she returned to the kitchen.

"Where do you eat your own meal?" he asked when she eventually placed the cheese board in front of him.

"With Nikon and Chloe in the kitchen. I shall never learn Greek if I don't try to talk to people."

He nodded, then grinned at her. "Of course. When you eat alone, you talk to yourself in your own language."

She flushed as she remembered the occasions when he had overheard her mutterings.

"Perhaps in due course I might learn to chatter to myself in Greek."

"Good idea!" he agreed.

She gave her attention to clearing away and stacking the plates and glasses on the tray. He had not bothered to ask her how she felt after this morning's encounter with the motor-boat or what injuries the doctor had diagnosed, or even if the doctor had called.

She was halfway to the door when he said, "Is your shoulder painful where the boat hit you this morning?"

"Not too bad," she replied lightly.

"I telephoned the doctor to ask him about your injuries. He told me they were not serious, but you might feel stiff and bruised within a day or two."

So he had checked up on the doctor's report. Out of sincere interest, or only to find if she might be exaggerating her aches and pains?

"So I thought we might perhaps give you a rest from cooking tomorrow," he continued. "You can arrange something simple for Nikon and the girl and then in the evening I'll take you to a place I know."

Her spirits soared at a ridiculous rate. "And lunch? Will you be in?"

"No. I have an appointment. You can probably fix up lunch for the three of you."

She picked up the tray which she had rested on a side table. "Thank you, Mr. Brendon," she said calmly, schooling her face into a formal expression, so that he should not criticise her again for a too-eager attitude.

But in the kitchen she could scarcely eat her own meal for the dancing excitement that coursed through her being. Presently she sobered, for the thought occurred to her that possibly his motive for taking her out to dinner was that he could stand no more of her cooking. True, she knew she was not in Caterina's class, but she could hardly be expected to have the housekeeper's long experience. Nikon and Chloe had pronounced the apple pie "Very good", but perhaps they were no more than polite.

Jacynth was relieved next day that some of her obligations had been lessened, for her right shoulder ached and as her typing took longer, she was glad not to spend too much time in the kitchen. But late in the afternoon when she went there to help a little with the evening meal for Nikon and Chloe, Nikon came to tell her that a visitor had called and would like to see Jacynth.

Her thoughts immediately veered to Ray. "I'll see him in a few minutes."

"A lady," Nikon informed her.

"Oh. Where have you taken her?"

He told her he had seated the lady in Jacynth's office.

She hurried out of the kitchen, wondering who the caller might be. Hermione Perandopoulos was standing at Jacynth's desk, glancing apparently idly at the document in the type-writer.

Jacynth gave the Greek girl a formal greeting, but Hermione did not return the salutation. "Miss Rowson – or whatever your name is – I understand that Mallory – Mr. Brendon – is without his cook."

"Yes. Caterina is ill."

"And you are taking her place?"

"I've been coping with a few meals, that's all," replied Jacynth mildly. "Won't you sit down, Miss Perandopoulos?"

Hermione ignored this invitation and took a few restless steps about the room. Then she glared at Jacynth. "Mallory knows perfectly well that at any time we could provide him with cooks or servants. There is simply no need for a typist to meddle in his household affairs."

"If Caterina is likely to be ill for some time, no doubt Mr. Brendon will get in touch with you," said Jacynth smoothly.

"I will not tolerate you any more, Miss Rowland!" Hermione's hazel eyes flashed with fury. "Ever since you came here, you've tried to insinuate yourself into Mallory's household. In fact, you've thrown yourself at him in the most shameless manner."

"That's not true!" contradicted Jacynth.

Hermione smiled scornfully. "Not true!" she repeated contemptuously. "Why, it's written all over you that you're in love – or fancy you are – with Mallory. I've already warned you how foolish you are, but you've taken no notice, so now I shall insist that Mallory gets rid of you."

"Perhaps Mr. Brendon might insist on choosing his own secretaries," Jacynth said.

"Do you really believe that he will listen to you and not to me?"

"I'm quite sure that you have great influence with him," Jacynth replied. Her mind was trying to find a way of getting rid of Hermione before Mallory could return. If the Greek girl were here when he came in, Jacynth could envisage several dismaying possibilities. Hermione might insist that Mallory dismiss his secretary on the spot. Even if he temporised, managed to calm down Hermione, it was very unlikely that he would fulfil his promise and take Jacynth out to dinner. His companion would undoubtedly be Hermione.

So now Jacynth adopted a bold course. "Miss Perandopoulos, please forgive me, but I have some work to finish tonight for Mr. Brendon, and then I have a dinner engagement."

Hermione stopped in mid-stride. "Really? So in spite of your supposed devotion to your employer, you have acquired some other men friends here?"

"Would that be unnatural?"

"Probably not in your case," retorted Hermione. "There are quite a number of young Englishmen here, and in fact, I understand from Mallory that you have a special friend."

Jacynth frowned. So Mallory had mentioned Ray, and Hermione was eager to seize on the connection.

"And I suppose you're now in a tearing hurry to finish your work and meet this young charmer tonight," Hermione smiled. "Perhaps you would do better to concentrate on him and dismiss all your romantic thoughts about Mallory. My advice would be for your own good."

Jacynth smiled tentatively. "I'm sure it would," she agreed. Oh, if only Hermione would leave now before further conversation led Jacynth into making promises that could not be fulfilled!

Hermione was gazing around the room. "You've no telephone in here, apparently. I want to make a call – to Mallory." She gave Jacynth an oblique glance that was a mixture of triumph and contempt.

"The only one is in Mr. Brendon's study." Jacynth accompanied the Greek girl, imagining that Hermione might know where Mallory would be at this hour.

"Where is he likely to be?" she asked.

Jacynth shook her head. "I don't know."

"Oh, come! Don't be evasive. Is he coming home to dinner?"

"No."

"Then I'll try two of the numbers I know." She glanced up at Jacynth. "My conversation will be private, so – if you don't mind?"

Reluctantly, Jacynth withdrew and returned to her own

room. She had never admitted strangers into Mallory's study, but Hermione was not actually in that category.

After a few minutes, Hermione came into Jacynth's room. "I couldn't get him at either number. So will you tell him I called? Ask him to phone me when he comes home. Better still, say that I shall expect him for dinner at the Grand Summer Palace."

"Certainly, Miss Perandopoulos." Jacynth was politeness itself, but could not restrain an inward delight that Mallory already had a prior engagement for dinner with herself.

Unless, she reflected dubiously after Hermione's departure, Mallory changed his mind and decided that the Greek girl had a greater claim on his companionship tonight.

As soon as he came in, Jacynth reported the gist of the interview with Hermione, omitting the more personal cut-and-thrusts.

"I'll telephone her straightaway," he said, and retired to his study. Jacynth waited in her "office", but after some twenty minutes she became impatient. Surely Mallory would come and tell her if he had altered tonight's arrangements. She picked up a file as a pretext and went along to his study.

She asked one or two business queries, then, taking her courage in her hands, said tentatively, "The arrangement you made – about dinner – does it still stand?"

He stared at her for a moment and colour flooded into her cheeks. "The arrangement? Of course."

"But Miss Perandopoulos?"

He waved his hand as though to brush away all importuning Greek girls. "Oh, I'm not a puppet on a string, ready to dance to any woman's tune. Go and get yourself ready, but don't dress up. It's a simple place where we're going."

She waited until she was safely outside the door before she allowed her face to relax into smiles of delight and, perhaps, a hint of triumph.

Mallory drove some miles along the coast, then turned inland to climb the hilly road through pines and cypress trees.

Jacynth schooled herself to sit sedately beside him, although sheer enchantment enveloped her in a blissful sense of gladness.

He stopped in the centre of a small village where a flight of wooden steps led to a long building shaded by a verandah. At the top of the steps Mallory was greeted by a burly man with enormous waxed moustaches and a beaming smile.

Jacynth was introduced to the man Andreas, who then led the way through the one-storey building to a large room built on the back. Several long tables were arranged around the sides, so that a clear space was left in the middle.

Jacynth understood at once that there would be a display of local dancing, but she was intrigued by the sight of saucers of honey accompanied by hunks of brownish bread set out along the wooden tables.

After a few minutes about a dozen people entered the room and began to choose their seats.

"We'd better choose our own," Mallory spoke to Jacynth, "or we shall lose the best places. *And* we were here first."

His smiling glance played havoc with her composure, as usual, but she followed him to the seats he selected.

"You must begin to eat," he whispered, as he broke his portion of bread and dipped pieces into the saucer of honey. Jacynth copied his example, and while she found the honey delightful and the bread much lighter in texture than it looked, she wondered what sort of dinner would follow this odd first course.

Mallory filled her glass from one of the bottles of local wine ranged along the table, and then helped himself to schnapps. It was not long before the dancers appeared, eight in local costume, to perform their sequence of the formal, graceful movements handed down by tradition. Mallory explained to Jacynth the meaning of the individual dances, that one was usually performed at weddings in honour of the bride, another might be for a joyous homecoming of a member of the family, or the birth of a child.

When the finale was reached, this with much stamping and

leaping by the men, Jacynth said, "Oh, I enjoyed all that very much."

"And the wine and honey?" Mallory queried. "This is the normal hospitality that any Greek household will show to strangers, bread and honey and wine. So now we'll go and have our dinner."

He escorted her, after prolonged farewells to Andreas, to another house in the village, where meals were served in a garden affording a wonderful panorama of the hills surrounding the village.

Mallory had warned her that the restaurant was only a simple place, but Jacynth thought the meal was superb, with fish in spicy sauces, delicious kebabs with aubergines, then the lightest of pastry cases filled with almond paste and raisins.

"You would hardly expect such a meal in so tiny a village," she said to Mallory.

"Oh, Georgy is very proud of his cooking. He goes in to Rhodes market every day and buys all his stuff absolutely fresh."

"As Nikon likes to do."

"That reminds me. – Caterina will be coming home in a couple of days' time, so you'll be out of your kitchen job."

She gave him a questioning glance. "Won't she need a few days at home for rest before she's pitchforked into the work of the household?"

He nodded. "She can take it easy for a while. She has that girl there to help her."

Jacynth put down her wineglass deliberately. "It may not be my place to speak, but I feel that you impose too much on Caterina."

"Really?" His lifted eyebrows almost daunted her, but she was determined to strike a blow for Caterina.

"Yes. She's on the go from morning till night, coping with all that housework as well as all the cooking, even though Nikon does the marketing."

"She's never complained."

"You know perfectly well that she would rather drop down dead in her kitchen than complain."

He rested his chin on the palm of his hand and stared at her across the table, making it difficult for her to sustain his gaze.

"But you would never put up with such a tyrannical employer?" he taunted.

"My case is different. I'm usually sitting down to the job, but Caterina is on her feet most of the day."

"And what do you suggest? How shall I arrange my household?"

"Well, perhaps you could keep the girl Chloe. I know she came in only temporarily, but Caterina could do with help in the rest of the house. Then she wouldn't get so tired standing to do the cooking."

"In future, I shall make no demands on her at all. I'll have the simplest meals, omelettes, bread and cheese, so no elaborate cooking will have to be done for me. As for other people in the house, they must arrange with Caterina for themselves." He gave her a dark, mischievous look and his eyes were dancing.

"Even that wouldn't please Caterina. She likes cooking a variety of dishes and gets cross when sometimes all her efforts are wasted."

"I must bear in mind all you say." Now he was laughing at her, but she did not mind, for she felt that his attitude at this moment was more congenial than usual.

"If Caterina is soon coming home, then will it be necessary to accept the offer made by Miss Perandopoulos to borrow a cook?"

"I think that's hardly likely. That would put Caterina's nose out of joint – and possibly yours?" In almost a split second, his manner had changed and become cold and sardonic.

"Probably I shouldn't have mentioned the subject," she said as coolly as she could, although she was raging inwardly and calling herself several sorts of fool for having meddled in his household concerns.

"In any case, I'm shortly joining Hermione and her father

for a cruise on their yacht, so Caterina will have an easier time while I'm away."

So shall I, she thought. I might need a quiet period to settle myself without these anguished adjustments to the man's moods.

Yet at the end of the evening he seemed to have recovered a more lighthearted attitude. When she stepped out of the car outside the door of the Villa Kalakos, she thanked him for a very pleasant evening. "Not only the dinner, but the dancing at that other place."

"Who knows what my motives might have been!" he answered. "Perhaps it was the thought of my own digestion – and a relief from your cooking!"

She was tempted to fling at him that he could always avail himself of Hermione's offer and accept one of her chefs, but that would have been foolhardy and she went up to her room, content with the thought that in spite of Hermione's invitation to dinner, he had fulfilled his promise to herself. That was at least a small, but not insignificant, victory.

CHAPTER EIGHT

DURING Mallory's absence on the Perandopoulos yacht, Jacynth was glad that she had little time to brood over what might be happening between Mallory and Hermione. He had left her an enormous amount of work and pages of instructions, but there were situations which might arise where she could use her own initiative, he told her. He entrusted her with keys to his desk and impressed on her that on no account was she to tell anyone that he had gone cruising.

"Just say that I'm away for a few days, take whatever messages are given and leave it at that."

Caterina was back and declared that she was quite well, but Jacynth persuaded her to accept Chloe's help in the house.

"Then all you have to do is the cooking and you can rest part of the day," advised Jacynth.

Caterina's smile lit up her gaunt face. "You are a kind girl," she murmured in Greek.

Sara had written that she and David would be coming to Rhodes at the end of the week and would be staying at the Mediterranean Hotel.

"Let me know if you don't want to see David and I'll see that he's out of the way," wrote Sara.

Jacynth replied that there was no need and she would be delighted to see them both.

She arranged her work for Mallory so that she could take all the afternoon and evening of the day she was to meet the couple.

Sara looked radiantly happy, and now Jacynth found she could look at David and see in him only the handsome husband of her cousin.

Sara plied her with questions about the job and Jacynth's employer. "How old is he?"

"Thirty-two."

"Oh, I'd imagined him more in his forties, perhaps. He treats you well?"

Jacynth smiled. "Very well – as long as I satisfy him in the work I do."

"It's rather an odd set-up, isn't it? Living in his house?"

"He prefers it that way. And of course it saves making journeys to and fro to an office."

"He's away now, you say," pursued Sara, with a smile. "I'd have liked to meet him."

"He's travelling about and will be away for a week or more." Jacynth was undecided whether she wanted Sara to meet Mallory. Her cousin's sharp eyes might detect that Jacynth's interest in her employer was not entirely limited to his business concerns. "I can take you to the house where I live, if you want to be assured that it's a respectable place," she added now, laughing.

"Might be a good idea," agreed Sara. After a pause she asked, "Have you made any friends on the island?"

"Well, no," replied Jacynth. "Working in the house I don't meet many people, but I met a young man at the airport when I came here and he's here on business sometimes, so we go out together occasionally."

David suggested they might go to the Sound and Light programme in the old city that night. "Would your friend care to join us? I know it's short notice, but perhaps you can telephone?"

Actually, Jacynth was reluctant to issue invitations to Ray on her own behalf, especially after that last encounter on the deserted beach, but she realised that a foursome would be more satisfactory than a threesome with Sara and David.

Ray was delighted to be asked, although he already had an engagement, he said, but would forgo that for the pleasure of being with Jacynth.

After dinner at Sara's hotel, the three met Ray at the entrance to the gardens from which the Sound and Light spectacle could be viewed. A small open-air amphitheatre provided an excellent view of the old walls and battlements which would be illuminated.

Jacynth was enthralled by the historical commentary and skilful lighting to accompany it, but towards the end, she became aware of Ray's boredom.

"Not really up my street," he confessed when the four were on the way out. "I'm all for everything modern and up-to-date."

On the other hand, David in his profession of architect was also keenly interested in archaeology and had visited sites in Greece and Crete.

"You must go to Lindos while you're here," Jacynth suggested, remembering the happy day she had spent there with Mallory.

During the rest of the time while Sara and David were in Rhodes, Jacynth managed to arrange her own work so that she could spend free time with them on some of the days.

Sara very much wanted to see the Villa Kalakos and the conditions in which Jacynth worked, so Jacynth arranged for the others to come one morning.

"I apologise for not offering lunch, but Caterina, the housekeeper, has been ill and if she knows there are visitors, she'll take special trouble to provide a very elaborate meal. Come about eleven and I'll have coffee and cakes ready."

After a short tour of inspection over the house, Sara pronounced herself satisfied that her cousin was working in reasonably comfortable circumstances. Jacynth had not entered Mallory's study and of course made no mention of the locked room. David was fascinated by the windmill and explored the interior.

"All these old windmills ought to be preserved, instead of most of them being knocked down when new hotels are built," he said. "This one could do with a small amount of restoration and your boss could make it quite a showplace."

Jacynth laughed. "I'll pass on your instructions."

On their last evening in Rhodes before they left for some of the other Greek islands, Sara and David invited Jacynth and

Ray to dinner at their hotel. During the meal Jacynth examined her emotions towards David and was gratified to find that she could look at him without a tremor of excitement. She could even take the utmost pleasure in the fact that he adored Sara and that her cousin, radiantly beautiful with her red-gold hair and dark violet eyes, had chosen this man out of all the throng who were attracted to her. Jacynth sincerely hoped that Sara and David would share a mutual happiness for all their lives.

In the few moments when she and Sara were alone while the two men had strolled off to the hotel terrace, Sara said quietly, "This man Ray – are you fond of him, Jacynth?"

"Why? Does it look as if I am?"

Sara frowned slightly. "No, perhaps not."

"I'm not making that mistake again," Jacynth reassured her cousin. "I've learned not to confuse infatuation with love."

Sara looked across at Ray's back as he stood with David. "He's not right for you, dear," she whispered. "Find other friends and don't let him think he can count on you."

Jacynth smiled. "Sara, it's sweet of you to care about me, but I'm very happy here, and I count Ray as no more than an acquaintance."

"He's a phoney," was Sara's assessment. "There's no solid core of kindness in him. He's shallow and would send anyone to the wall for the sake of his ambitions."

"You *have* summed him up," said Jacynth, laughing, "but you've no need to worry." Not about *that* man, she added to herself. It was perhaps fortunate that the two men returned before Sara could delve into Jacynth's emotional relationship with her employer.

After Sara's departure with David, Ray seemed anxious to renew his friendship with Jacynth, offering to take her to places whenever he was in Rhodes and had time.

Jacynth excused herself from immediate arrangements on the ground that she had already spent time with her cousin and her husband and must now make up on Mallory's work.

"But I'll come out again when I can manage it," she agreed,

placatingly, for in some ways she liked Ray, although she could see some of his most glaring faults.

When Mallory returned from the yachting trip, he seemed more than usually pleased with life. He announced to Jacynth that he had been invited on the yacht to meet several highly-placed men who needed his advice on investing in property deals. Mr. Perandopoulos, Hermione's father, had introduced them to Mallory and several very profitable arrangements were likely to result.

"A good place, a yacht sailing some distance from the land, for discussions like this," he observed.

"But surely the yacht has radio connections?" queried Jacynth.

"Naturally, but it's more difficult to make excuses about seeing someone else, another partner or director, as the case may be. Decisions have to be made on the strength of personal discussion."

She wondered what sort of "personal discussions" he might also have had with Hermione. As two or three days went by and there was no mention of Mallory dismissing Jacynth, the latter assumed that he had not listened very attentively to Hermione's demands for sacking her.

Then one evening Hermione called, ostensibly to deliver some confidential documents from her father, but stayed to dinner which Caterina served on the covered terrace outside the drawing-room windows.

Jacynth, who had eaten her own dinner in her accustomed place in her office-sitting-room, was surprised when Caterina came in with a message that Mr. Brendon wanted her to join him on the terrace.

So this was the crunch! Hermione had renewed her demands and now she was here in the house and Mallory would have no option but to comply.

Jacynth went slowly to what she regarded as her doom. Hermione was lounging gracefully in a long chair close enough to Mallory's own for her to stretch out a hand and clasp one of his.

161

Mallory rose and pulled up another chair for Jacynth. "Miss Rowan plays the piano," he said chattily to Hermione. Turning towards Jacynth, he asked, "Will you play something for us now?"

His suggestion was so contrary to what she had expected that for a moment or two words failed her. Then she recovered part of her composure. "I'm afraid I'm very much out of practice," she apologised.

She was furious with Mallory for exposing her to Hermione's ridicule. In any case, what did these two want from her? A gentle serenade to provide a background for their intimate conversation? Jacynth would see them hanged first before she would comply with his request.

"Perhaps some other time," she now added with a smile at Hermione.

"You have great faith in the future," retorted Hermione in a fierce undertone.

Mallory had lit another cigar and now sat down. "We were discussing this house and what to make of it," he said to Jacynth. "Until now I've rented it from the Italian owner, the woman who used to live in it. Now she wants to sell and has offered me the first refusal."

"It would be a poor bargain, whatever the price," declared Hermione.

"I don't think so. It would need completely redecorating," observed Mallory.

"Nonsense. This villa is simply not worth redecorating," Hermione said emphatically. "You know that my father has half a dozen houses here in Rhodes and every one of them much better than this. Surely the best plan would be to let the Italian woman sell the villa and the site to one of your hotel companies. You could probably buy it quite cheaply for that purpose."

"That has always been a possibility, of course, and she is well aware of it," he agreed.

"Even the garden is shabby and your swimming-pool a joke," continued Hermione. "One thing you could get rid of is that dreadful old windmill cluttering up the space."

"Oh, no!" exclaimed Jacynth involuntarily, and the other two turned to glance at her. "I'm sorry, I shouldn't have spoken, but I – I like the windmill."

Hermione smiled contemptuously. "I'm surprised to find you in favour of anything so antiquated, but then of course whether Mallory keeps it or not hardly concerns you, does it?"

Jacynth subsided with a muttered, "As you say", but then she caught Mallory's eye and saw his faint nod of approval. At least, she supposed it was approval. Was he then egging her on to spar with Hermione?

After a while, Hermione rose. "Take me round these well-laid-out grounds of yours," she commanded Mallory. "Possibly a new hotel might make a splendid feature of your precious windmill."

She threw Jacynth a triumphant glance as she linked her arm with Mallory's. Naturally Jacynth did not expect to be invited to such a tête-à-tête and was puzzled as to why Mallory had asked her out here in the first place, apart from asking her to play the piano.

So now she went into the drawing room, where the grand piano offered a challenge. Impulsively, she sat on the long brocaded stool, lifted the keyboard fall and propped up the lid. She played a few chords softly to flex her fingers, then began a Debussy Arabesque, but she was not in the mood for gentleness and chose a Chopin Polonaise, all fiery brilliance. Finally she played the Revolutionary Study, which more nearly matched the indignation she felt after her encounter with Hermione.

She banged out the final chords, then became aware that Hermione had entered the room through the french windows, with Mallory close behind her.

"So you really can play," was Hermione's cool comment. "I thought perhaps you could manage only a few waltzes on a schoolroom level. I apologise for doubting you."

Hermione's apologies were no more than tissue paper, but

Jacynth whirled round on the stool. "As I said, I'm out of practice. Plenty of wrong notes – if you detected them," she added, as a barb. "And my repertoire of works I can play from memory is not very large."

She rose. "If you'll excuse me, I'll go along to the kitchen and see if Caterina needs any help." She escaped from the room before Mallory could make any further requests, although she knew that Caterina would have finished her work in the kitchen long since.

Next day Mallory again spoke of the villa. "As Miss Perandopoulos points out, there are many other villas on the island – and elsewhere in Greece or other islands – that I could make into a home eventually."

Jacynth refused to look at him in case he might read the anguished despair in her eyes. So he was now thinking of marrying Hermione and settling down somewhere. True, there would be plenty of the Perandopoulos establishments, but naturally Mallory would want one house he could call his own.

"The woman owner now needs the cash. She's had a tragic life in some ways. Husband killed in the war, one of her sons lost in an air crash and another, a young boy, died when he was about fifteen."

"How unhappy her life must have been," murmured Jacynth sympathetically.

"Of course the boy's room would have to be opened and cleared out," Mallory continued. "That locked room along the corridor – that was her younger son's room and she wanted it kept as he left it."

So that was the secret of that locked room!

"But I'm glad you like the windmill," he added. "Perhaps one day I'll have it cleared out and renovated."

"And I'm pleased that you don't want to demolish it," she answered.

"Perhaps we all demolish too much – and then don't know what we really want to build in place."

He went out of the room before Jacynth could fathom the

meaning of this cryptic remark.

A few days later Ray telephoned, asking if Jacynth could spare time for a steamer trip along the coast next day.

"It means a whole day, so tell your boss you must leave early and get back late," he advised.

Mallory was not in at that moment, but Jacynth replied, "All right, Ray, and thank you. I'll be there."

"Eight o'clock at the harbour. I'll meet you down there opposite the Market Hall and we'll find the ship."

As she put down the receiver, Jacynth began to regret her easy acquiescence in the plan. She was not so worried about taking the day off as to the wisdom of further excursions with Ray. She had not meant to encourage him after Sara's visit, but she was committed now.

Mallory made no difficulty when she explained that she was quite up to date with the work, unless he urgently needed her tomorrow.

His gleaming eyes disconcerted her, especially when he said lightly, "I need you every day – but you can go off and enjoy yourself."

I need you every day. The words rattled in her brain, but of course he didn't mean them in the way she longed for him to need her, as a person and not as a fairly efficient secretary.

The steamer trip was scheduled to sail down the north-west coast of Rhodes and then close to the island of Alimia.

"Do we land there?" asked Jacynth when she and Ray were seated on the upper deck.

"Don't think so. I believe it's a wild sort of place. I thought I could have a look at it and I might make a special journey another time and see what I can pick up in the way of pottery or other lines."

By now Jacynth was accustomed to the fact that usually Ray had a twofold purpose whenever he proposed a jaunt. It was never merely for pleasure.

Jacynth gave herself up to the enjoyment of the day, watching the rocky coastline of Rhodes slide by, seeing the clusters of white houses indicating small towns.

After lunch, which proved to be a delicious assortment of fish with salad, followed by pastries and cheese, the steamer veered northwards towards another island, Symi, close to the Turkish coast. Jacynth saw from the map symbols that here were Byzantine and medieval sites.

"I should love to explore this island," she said. "Maybe later on I can find out where a steamer calls there."

Ray laughed at her with some indulgence. "You're always wrapped up in the past. Think of the future."

"I don't know how you can travel about Greece and the islands and not be moved by all that they can show of their wonderful past," she retorted.

"The past is all very well, but it doesn't provide me with my keep for the years to come."

Jacynth sighed and concentrated on the colourful rocky coast of Symi, vowing that when she had the chance, she would spend a long holiday pottering about all these little islands.

It was some time later when both she and Ray became aware of the changed rhythm of the ship, which had slowed speed. Passengers began to ask each other what was the matter, deckhands ran about apparently engaged on urgent tasks.

"Engine failure, I think," commented Ray. "But they're sure to repair the fault, whatever it is, and we'll be on our way."

But it soon became obvious to Jacynth that the ship had ceased to make way and was slowly drifting in the direction of the Turkish coast.

"Why don't they put back to Symi?" muttered Ray irritably. "They'll soon be in Turkish waters at this rate."

Apparently it proved impossible to turn back to Symi or any other Greek territory. An officer came along the decks informing people quietly that there was no danger, but that the steamer would have to land at some point in Turkey.

"Got your passport?" asked Ray of Jacynth, who nodded. It was only a fluke that she had put it into her handbag this morning.

The more worrying problem for her was a very late return to Rhodes. Mallory would expect her home at a reasonable hour.

Eventually two tugs came out from the shore and the steamer was guided into a tiny harbour, where all passengers were ordered to disembark.

"Why on earth couldn't they have got tugs from a Greek port?" asked Ray. Other men were echoing the same idea, but a seaman explained that none were apparently available and the captain could not risk his ship grounding on the rocks.

The formalities were long and complicated. Jacynth had imagined that a show of passports would be all that was necessary, but everyone had to fill in long forms, giving detailed information as to residence, occupation, nationality and so on.

"When do we leave here?" Jacynth wanted to know.

"How should I know?" rasped Ray. "You're safe on land, anyway."

Then an official came into the large room to which the passengers had been confined and announced that a steamer would return them to Rhodes tomorrow morning.

"Tomorrow?" gasped Jacynth.

Ray shrugged his shoulders and grinned. "Thank your lucky stars you're with me, instead of at the mercy of—" He broke off. "Why, this is almost where we came in, you and I. Remember? At the airport at Athens, when we lost the plane."

"I remember," she said grimly. That adventure had done her no good at all with Mallory and this one could probably have unpleasant consequences.

In due course the women and children passengers were taken to a separate room where a simple meal was provided; bowls of soup with bread. Some of the women complained that the food was not much of a dinner which they needed, but Jacynth considered that the Turkish officials were doing everything possible for a number of chance passengers who had not been expected. Later in the evening rugs and blankets were handed to the mothers with children and the uniformed men were apologetic that they could not provide for everyone.

Jacynth made the best of the situation by pillowing her head on her cardigan and trying to sleep, even in fitful dozes.

In the morning, the passengers were given hot coffee and biscuits and at nine o'clock were shepherded to a small steamer which would take them to Rhodes.

Jacynth soon found Ray on the deck and asked how he had fared.

"Terrible. Hardly any food and nowhere to sleep."

"What did you expect?" she queried sharply. "A four-course dinner and a comfortable sofa to sleep on?"

Ray looked down at her and yawned. "The affair hasn't improved your temper. It wasn't my fault that the ship broke down."

"I'm not blaming you for anything. I just wish it hadn't happened at this particular time." If Mallory had been away from the villa, it would not have mattered, but now she saw clearly that the fragile harmony that existed between her and her employer was likely to be snapped irrevocably.

It was perhaps fortunate that she had at that moment little idea of how devastating the storm would be.

CHAPTER NINE

"How can you blame me for the ship breaking down?" Jacynth was more angry now than she had ever imagined. Mallory was taking a fiendish delight in proving that she was nothing but a cheap, wanton girl who seized any opportunity of staying out at nights with her men friends.

"I'm not yet convinced that you were on the steamer at all," he hurled at her, his eyes blazing.

"You can check that with the Turkish authorities. I filled in a lengthy form and signed my name to it."

"Hermione was right when she said—"

"I'm well aware of Miss Perandopoulos's views," Jacynth interrupted, her discretion thrown to the winds. "Ever since she met me, she's been trying to persuade you to sack me, send me back to England, anywhere, so long as I have no contact with you. Now she's succeeded. The perfect excuse for sacking me has dropped right into your lap."

"Who said I was sacking you?" he demanded.

Jacynth glared at him across the desk. At first she had tried to explain rationally and quietly the sequence of last night's events, but gradually the interview had developed into a shouting match until they were both facing each other across three feet of mahogany, Mallory's dark eyes by turn contemptuous or fiercely unbelieving, her own face flushed and her voice almost out of control.

"Do you really think I could go on working for an employer who takes the attitude you're taking?" she demanded.

"In that case, you're sacking yourself."

"In that case," she repeated mockingly, "you're finding it convenient to put the onus on me."

Now she was holding on with both hands to the edge of the desk. She was really burning her boats now. Mallory was not the man to capitulate, to withdraw his accusations that she was just another permissive girl with little sense of morality.

Suddenly Mallory sat down at his desk and ran his fingers through his thick, dark hair. The gesture, so familiar to her, almost demolished her resolution not to surrender; she wanted to run to him, crave his indulgence, beg him to let her stay, but she steeled herself to endure. What good could come of staying in his employ now? She would always feel ashamed, humiliated, even though she had not committed a sin other than being shut up in a Turkish Customs shed all night.

"I think it's time to put an end to all this," he said coldly, as he drew his cheque book out of the drawer. She watched him for a few moments as he began to write a cheque.

As he said, this was really the end. He tossed the cheque towards her.

"I've added an extra amount to compensate for the lack of notice – on either side," he added, with a significant glance at her. "There's also enough for your air fare home."

Jacynth picked up the cheque and glanced at the amount, generous by any standards. But the size of the sum only served to reawaken her fury. "I don't want any kind of bonus," she stormed. "I'm not accustomed to being bought off. Nor do I need the money for my air fare."

He raised his eyebrows. "Oh? Do you intend hitch-hiking back to England?"

"My methods of travel are my own business. For the present, I intend to stay in Rhodes."

"I see." He almost hissed the words at her as he came towards her, and for a wild, panic moment she thought he was going to take her by the shoulders and shake the life out of her. "You're going to stay here – with this man, who obviously means so much to you."

"He's always been willing to offer me a job here," she said shakily.

"How wise of you to provide yourself with a second

string! May I be permitted to ask where you will live? Or are you planning to share whatever accommodation he has?"

"My future is of no concern to you, Mr. Brendon," she flung at him, although her eyes were brimming with tears. He would never know how much she longed for her future to be his concern.

She pushed the cheque towards him. "Perhaps you could let me have one for the salary owing to me – and nothing more."

With cold deliberation he tore the first cheque into small pieces and let them drop from his fingers on to the desk. When he handed her the second cheque, he said maliciously, "Allow me to wish you success in your – new venture."

In her turn, she longed to tear this cheque into small pieces and fling them in his face, but that would have been a futile gesture, merely robbing herself of money she would need in the next week or two.

"I will finish the work outstanding," she said with as much dignity as she could muster.

"You will certainly not," he snapped. "I'd rather you left the house as soon as you can pack your belongings. I don't want to see you again."

"And I shall be glad to go!" Jacynth retorted defiantly.

But in her bedroom she collapsed on the bed and wept for sheer misery. That final lie had unnerved her, and if she had stayed another moment in Mallory's study, she would have completely disgraced herself by a torrent of weeping.

When she was calmer, she asked herself how she could go on loving so stubbornly a man firmly determined to believe the worst, even when all the circumstances yelled aloud that she was not to blame.

It took little time to pack her few belongings, but when she unhooked the beautiful tile plaque of the Prince of the Lilies, which Mallory had given her, her tears started afresh. The pottery vase portraying the Cupbearers, which Ray had given her, had caused no such flood of emotion. Perhaps one day she might be able to look on the tile plaque and remember without grief of an episode in her life and a man whose image would always remain in her mind.

When she went downstairs to say goodbye to Caterina and Nikon, she visited first her office-sitting-room and noticed immediately that all papers and files had been removed by Mallory. Only the covered typewriter remained; otherwise, all evidence of her occupation of the room had vanished.

Jacynth wished that she could as easily expunge Mallory from her immediate memory as he had evidently been able to do regarding herself. The slate was wiped clean.

She asked Nikon to order her a taxi, for she would not humble herself to ask Mallory to telephone for her. As the taxi drew away from the Villa Kalakos, Jacynth imagined that she saw Mallory's figure outside the windmill, but of course, that was merely wishful thinking playing tricks.

She instructed the taxi driver to take her to a small hotel along the coast road, one she had seen on her walks around. She checked in for two nights, saying she would stay longer if necessary and they had a room available.

Next she must see Ray and explain some of the situation. Out of bravado, she had told Mallory that she could easily work for Ray, but that would not be possible. She did not want to be employed by him and in close contact, nor could he yet afford her salary. At the same time, she must prevent him from trying to telephone her at the Villa Kalakos.

She went to a small café along the promenade and while she ate a light meal, worked out her finances. She calculated that her funds would cover moderate expenses for the next four weeks, but that would leave nothing for her air fare home. Alternatively, she could fly back to England within the next day or two and use the money that way. As a last resort, she could probably ask the company in London to send her an air ticket and she would repay them later. Even if Mallory was able to put in his side of the story first, the company would certainly not leave her stranded.

She knew the shop in the old town where Ray lodged and used the address for business transactions and it was late afternoon when she called. The owner, a young Greek, said that he believed Ray was in his room upstairs.

Jacynth paused outside the door indicated, for she heard the murmur of voices in the room. She knocked and waited, then knocked a second time. "Ray," she called. After a long pause, Ray opened the door. He was wearing a pair of shorts, the upper half of his body was bare and his hair stood up untidily.

Behind him through the open doorway, she caught a glimpse of a girl with long dark hair.

"Oh – er – Jacynth," murmured Ray, not exactly at ease. "I – I didn't expect you."

The girl edged through the doorway and hurried along the passage to another room.

"Oh, come in, Jacynth," Ray invited. "I'm all at sixes and sevens – taking a day off yesterday. By the way, how did your boss –?"

"Who was that girl?" Jacynth interrupted.

Ray stared back boldly. "That was Margarita. She's the sister of the fellow downstairs who owns the shop. She helps me a bit with typing and sorting out the orders and so on."

Jacynth gave him a level look, and he turned his head away. "Very lightly clad, even for hot weather?" The girl had plainly been wearing only a dressing wrap and nothing underneath.

"Look here, Jacynth, I'm not going to be bullied about what girl-friends I have."

"I've no intention of doing so," she answered crisply. "I only came to tell you that I've left the Villa Kalakos, so don't ring me there. I'm probably going home in a couple of days' time. Goodbye, Ray."

She was halfway down the stairs when she heard his voice. "Jacynth! Don't go, I can explain –!"

But she needed no explanations. She had done the wisest thing by saying that she might leave Rhodes in a couple of days. She hoped she could keep out of his way for at least the next week. All that she had wanted now was any help he could give her in recommending a room where she could lodge cheaply, instead of paying hotel prices.

She went through the old town, paused to watch the colony of cats near one of the gates, and chose a waterfront café to drink coffee while she reflected on her next move.

The alternatives were clear. Go home while she still had enough money for the air fare. Stay in Rhodes and try to find another job. She still had her work permit, but it would be difficult to explain leaving the employ of Mr. Mallory Brendon. Naturally, any prospective employer would demand a reference from him.

Her idle glance fell on a Greek newspaper left on a chair at another table. The headline mentioned "Kriti" and she picked up the paper. By now she could roughly follow the gist of the news and she read of the arrival of a French naval vessel at Heraklion and a Greek admiral paying a courtesy visit.

Crete! She could try her luck there, she supposed, and certainly she would be out of the way of both Ray and Mallory. Probably the cheapest method of travel would be by steamer. The Tourist Information Office was not far away and she walked along the street Alexandrou Papagou to the corner. The clerk gave her useful information about times of sailings and fares and she jotted down the particulars.

It was later that evening when in her hotel bedroom she was checking her available money that she discovered her work permit was missing. She hunted through her handbag and suitcases without success. She was sure that she had tucked the document inside her passport, but it was no longer there.

She bit her lip in vexation. She was not sure if the same document would be valid in Crete, but she would probably have to produce the old one from Rhodes if she wanted a job.

The only solution was to return to the Villa Kalakos, but she shrank from this prospect. She remembered that tomorrow Mallory had an appointment at Lindos in connection with the hotel there, so he would be away all day. If she could quietly ask Caterina to allow her to search for the permit, perhaps she could avoid another meeting with Mallory.

Jacynth chose about noon next day, and Caterina seemed delighted to see her. The housekeeper was only too ready to accompany the girl from room to room in the search for the missing permit. There was no trace in any of the dressing-table drawers. not anywhere in the office-sitting room which Jacynth had used.

"I must give it up and trust to luck," she said at last. Caterina begged her to stay to lunch if she would agree to eating in the kitchen, but before accepting, Jacynth asked casually if Mr. Brendon would be home to lunch.

"Not all day," muttered Caterina. "Not even to dinner."

So Jacynth was safe for an hour or two anyway. After lunch she wandered around the garden which Nikon now kept very tidy and then, on impulse, went into the old windmill. The door was still stiff and she had to ask Nikon to push it for her.

She perched herself on the millstone and pondered about the young Italian boy who had evidently used the mill as a refuge and a secret hiding place. Here were remnants of his possessions, the bagatelle board thick with dust, part of a tennis racket, a collapsed football and a bicycle pump rusty and broken.

She wondered what was in the locked room that his mother had preserved for so many years, but she would never know now, for even if Mallory bought the villa, Jacynth would be far away.

She now found an old exercise book with pages torn out, but what remained were covered in elegant Italian writing. A tender smile curved her lips, for she saw that the lines were verse.

A sudden noise caused her to look up sharply and she saw the vague outline of a man's figure silhouetted against the doorway. Nikon wanted her to leave so that he could shut the door. The figure advanced and she saw with consternation that it was Mallory.

The exercise book fell from her grasp as she backed away from him, her heart thudding in dismay. What unlucky chance had brought him here when he should have been far away in another part of the island?

"So you came back," he said quietly.

"Yes. I've mislaid my work permit and I had to come today to try to find it."

"And did you expect to find the permit here in the windmill?"

"Of course not. Caterina helped me to search my bedroom and the office – but – "

"With no result?"

"No. It seems to have disappeared. I came in here out of curiosity." She was feeling slightly calmer now, but she could not see his face, for he was against the light. Yet there was menace in his attitude and in his voice.

"And you need that work permit if you're going to your boy-friend." He had taken a couple of steps towards her and she backed still farther against the wall. Suddenly he was holding her shoulders in an iron grip and his face was only inches from her own. "Did you really think I would let you go and work for that worthless go-getter?"

"I've changed my mind," she managed to whisper. "I'm going to Crete to try for a job there."

"You're not going to Crete or anywhere else," Mallory said emphatically. He shook her shoulders angrily so that her head was thrust to and fro. Then she was held against him and his lips were on hers, crushing her into a wild surrender that was ecstasy itself.

"I can't let you go, Jacynth," he whispered. "I thought I could, but – it's impossible – you've become essential to me."

Now he held her more gently, cradling her head against his shoulder, murmuring endearments in Greek which she longed to have translated, but which she feared to ask at this blissful moment in case the magic spell were broken. He kissed her hair, her cheekbones, her neck and again her lips.

He pulled her down on to the millstone and sat with her held close to his side. "I've had no time for marriage and if I may say so, there have been one or two women who would have willingly said 'yes' if I asked them."

Jacynth's thoughts flew to Hermoine who was surely one of those women.

"But I prided myself on being invulnerable. Maybe, at some later date, I'd find a woman whom I'd want to spend my remaining years."

"And have you found her?" asked Jacynth softly.

"No."

She pulled away from him in shock, but he drew her closer to him and kissed her. "No. I couldn't wait that length of time. You came – the English girl – "

"The wrong one, you said," she reminded him.

"And you were!" Again the shock of puzzlement assailed her. "You upset all my normal plans, you just sailed through my defences. At first, I worked you to death, hoping you'd give up and go home of your own accord and leave me in peace. But you were tough. I think I began to fall in love with you when you answered back. Oh, I told myself I was merely an impressionable fool, but that morning when the boat hit you when I was skiing, I knew then that I couldn't bear to lose you."

For a moment Jacynth sat in silent enchantment. Never in her wildest imagination had she been able to conjure up such rapturous moments as these.

"I was told before I came that you were quite irresistible." she murmured.

"And did you resist?"

She laughed softly. "Not very much. I'd lost my willpower very soon."

"Yet you allowed that English fellow to take you out and about and make love to you – " he accused.

"Never. No more than a kiss or two that meant nothing."

"I hated the sound of him. The only time I met him I wanted to knock him down, boot him out of my house."

"Poor Ray. He wouldn't have deserved that," she smiled.

"Why not? He was an intruder. Then I began to wonder how many other English or Greek men you'd met on the island."

"As you admitted, you kept my nose to the grindstone too much for me to make many other friends."

"That was intentional. I made extra work for you, so that I could keep you under my eye – or at least know that you were slaving away at the typwriter in my absence."

"Tyrant!" she gibed.

After a pause he said, "I really don't know why I should love you so distractedly. You have none of the qualities I'd look for in a wife."

"Thank you," she said, bridling.

He laughed delightedly and hugged her. "That's it! You're fiery and peppery instead of being gracious and composed."

"Is that what you wanted?"

"I thought I did – but you changed all my priorities. I'd been imagining a kind of etiquette-book hostess to entertain my guests, someone impossibly elegant to take to receptions. And here you are, with your tousled blonde hair and scuffing about in a windmill and – "

When he paused she twisted to look up at him and try to see his eyes. "Say it, Mallory."

"Say what?"

"That you love me. I want to hear the words."

"I've yet to hear you say the words."

"Of course I love you, Mallory. I ached for you, and when you sent me away, I was desolate."

"I watched you go," he said sombrely, "and wondered if I'd ever see you again. I hoped you'd come back within a day or two asking for your work permit – unless you were stupid enough to send for it by post."

"Why?"

"Because I hid it. I took it out of your drawer. Even then, I couldn't be sure if you were really going to work for some-one else. You might not have needed it."

As the realisation slowly dawned on her that he had contrived in a gloriously underhand way to ensure her return if he could, she lifted her face and kissed him. "A diabolical scheme," she whispered, "but it worked."

"And now you'll never need the work permit again. Now, let's go somewhere less dusty than this place."

He lifted her down from the millstone and she clung to him for a moment, as he kissed her with tenderness.

When they emerged into the sunlight, she asked about Hermione. "I thought you would marry her."

Mallory smiled. "Hermione is very attractive, but not to me. She'll always be surrounded by a cluster of men, of whom one will possibly be her husband. I couldn't have played that rôle. I want to be unique – in my wife's eyes."

Jacynth saw that his dark jacket was smeared with dust from the mill and she dusted some of it away with her hand – as a wife might do. "How did you know I was in the windmill to-day?"

"I asked Caterina to telephone me if you came back at any time and then Nikon told me where you were."

"But you were supposed to be in Lindos today," she pointed out.

"Mercy! Am I to be bullied already because I choose to change my mind? What have I let myself in for?"

She linked her arm in his and skipped happily alongside him towards the villa.

A few yards from the terrace outside the drawing-room he paused and gazed critically at the villa. "Will you like living here, Jacynth? Or will you want something more stylish, imposing?"

She shook her head. "Anywhere with you will always suit me, but actually I like the villa."

"We could make a few alterations when I buy it. We shall have all the rooms available, for the Italian woman won't expect me to keep her son's room intact."

"There's also that other little room across the hall where there's so much furniture you can hardly get in."

CHAPTER TEN

LATER that afternoon Mallory drove her to the hotel where she had engaged a room, so that she could repack her belongings and return with them to the villa. As she unpacked in her old room, stowing her clothes in the wardrobe her glance fell on the double bed which she had always occupied and she wondered — But that was all far ahead, and although she felt dizzy with joy, she must really bring herself down to earth.

Caterina cooked a special dinner which Mallory had ordered and which was served in the formal dining room by candlelight. There was champagne and at one juncture, Mallory rang for Caterina and Nikon to come and join in a toast on the engagement of the master and the English secretary. Caterina was all beams and smiles and whispered something to Jacynth that was undoubtedly uncomplimentary to Miss Perandopoulos.

After dinner Mallory asked Jacynth to play the piano in the drawing-room. "But not Chopin's Revolutionary, I hope," he added.

She laughed. "No, something more gentle. Perhaps I'll play the Revolutionary only if I'm boiling over with anger."

"When you do, I shall clear out of the house," he warned her.

She played Debussy and a Spanish dance by Granados, and Mallory came behind her and leaned her head against him, so that she lost the thread of the composition and he picked up her fingers and kissed them one by one.

She asked him later about his secretarial work. "There's no reason why I can't continue to do it, is there?"

"For the time being, of course. Then I shall have to get a new secretary."

"One sent out from England?" she queried.

"Why?" His eyes danced with the light that she had always hoped to see in them. "Jealous?"

"You seem rather susceptible to girls from England. There was Diana – "

He looked smug. "I was wondering when you'd mention her."

"Did you like her?"

"As a girl – or a secretary?"

"Both. You were anxious to have her sent out again."

Mallory grinned. "I thought I might make you jealous of her, so I pretended she was quite my ideal. I asked for her because she was reasonably satisfactory and efficient and I didn't want to be burdened with a nitwit."

"Was that how I appeared to you at first? A nitwit?"

"You know perfectly well that I was entirely thrown off my balance."

So for the next few days Jacynth continued working for Mallory as before. Yet, of course, the situation was now quite different, for he had brought a selection of engagement rings for her choice and now she wore a handsome sapphire and diamond cluster on her third finger. But it was not only the wearing of a ring. The whole atmosphere had changed, and Jacynth had never realised how young and boyish Mallory could be.

Once or twice he took her out to dinner and on one occasion the American business man. Mr. Carlyon, had come up to congratulate Mallory.

"I said this was the year when you'd give up your bachelor life and settle down," he said, glancing genially at Jacynth, who remembered that he had prophesied a different partnership for Mallory.

Suddenly Jacynth's whole world exploded and fell in ruins. One morning Mallory was in his study when Jacynth entered and she saw at once that he was in a towering temper.

"How could you do this, Jacynth?" he stormed at her.

"Do what? What is it?"

"This." He handed her a Greek newspaper and pointed to a column on the financial page. "If you can't read it, I'll tell you. Perandopoulos has secured the contract that I was just about to sign. He's undercut our bid by two million."

Jacynth raised a white, puzzled face towards him. "But – but – I don't understand," she stammered. "If his bid were lower, then – "

"His initial bid was much higher. I know that. But somehow, *somehow*, he managed to get hold of our figures, slice off a couple of million and put in his own tender. No one knew our figures except two people – you and me."

"But how could I have disclosed them to anyone? I don't even know Mr. Perandopoulos."

"Plenty of other people do, and I should hardly expect you to act directly. That information was worth quite a few thousand drachmas. I don't doubt that this boy-friend of yours could do with some extra capital if he's setting up on his own. Between the pair of you, he's probably managed to make a handsome start."

When the full meaning dawned on Jacynth, she became ice-cold. "How dare you accuse me of using your business secrets? Is that the sort of girl you think I am?"

"You knew that Perandopoulos was our rival in this particular deal."

"Yes. But it wouldn't occur to me to sell information either to him or through any kind of intermediary. As for Ray being able to dispose of it to anyone as important as Mr. Perandopoulos, that's quite absurd."

Mallory paced the room. "I just can't see any other way in which the information could leak."

A sudden flash of vision came into Jacynth's mind. She remembered when Hermione had called and glanced at the work in the typewriter. Subsequently, she had been alone in Mallory's study on the pretext of telephoning him. How much could she have examined the files and documents in his desk?

"Well? Have you anything to say?" he now demanded.

How could she say that she suspected Hermione, who would

naturally deny any such charge?

He sat down at his desk and put his head into his hands. "Jacynth, I trusted you – I'd have trusted you with my life." After a few moments he straightened up. "It isn't really the loss of business that matters. It's you." He laughed mockingly. "I can see now that all along I've been taken for a ride. You and your boy-friend had it all planned, didn't you? You were to pretend you loved me – "

"I didn't pretend, I do love you."

"Then why? – oh, it doesn't make sense."

"No, it doesn't make sense to me either," she said coldly, although she was fiercely angry. "Here is your ring." She pulled it off her finger slowly and laid it on his blotter-pad. "I'll bring you the keys I have of your desk and the safe. Perhaps you'd like to check first and then lock up all the other confidential documents. I don't want to be accused of further thefts!"

She rushed out of the study before she could burst into tears. She must control herself, even though her heart was breaking into a hundred pieces. When she returned with the keys, Mallory was not there and a few moments later, she heard the sound of his car driving away.

Jacynth sat down in his chair, closed her eyes in misery. She should have known that such heights of joyous happiness could not last. One cannot remain on the peak and the descent into the abyss is full of terrors.

She became aware of the telephone ringing and she picked it up mechanically.

"Oh, that you, Jacynth?" Ray was calling. "Oh, good. Look, I wanted to explain about that other day when you called, but – "

"It doesn't matter, Ray. Forget it."

He laughed. "Forget it? I daresay you can. I've just heard that you're going to marry the great tycoon. You've done very well for yourself, haven't you? Stringing me along with all those tales of how you hated him and he worked you so hard and all that. Oh, well, enjoy your bargain. Good luck to you if you can make a go of it. Incidentally, I might know in the future where to come for a small loan, perhaps? If I needed a bit more capital? How about it?"

She jammed down the receiver. It was ironic that Ray should wish her good luck at the very time when her relationship with Mallory had so utterly crashed into destruction.

She went up to her bedroom, wondering what on earth she could do now. She could still go to Crete, she supposed. Mallory would have to give her the work permit if she demanded it.

Once again wearily she began to pack her suitcases, but this time she left the tiled plaque of the Prince of the Lilies conspicuously on the dressing table. She wanted nothing more to remind her of Mallory. She would go right out of his life, as no doubt he had already thrust her out of his own.

This time she would not ask Nikon to get a taxi. She used the telephone in Mallory's study for the last time and when she saw the taxi arrive, she carried the cases out of the front door quietly and could not even bear to take a backward glance of the Villa Kalakos, although she caught a glimpse of the windmill.

A ship would sail for Crete tonight, she found, and in the meantime, she would sit in a café. Her mind was numb with the morning's events and as the day wore on she tried to make her mind a complete blank. She thought of her own childhood, traced her school progress, remembered holidays, her music exams, anything to shut out this aching bewilderment that enveloped her.

She was glad when at last it was time to board the ship. Then she realised that in her anguish, she had again forgotten the matter of the work permit. She did not know where Mallory had hidden it and was too depressed at the time to look for it. Never mind. Permit or no permit, she was embarked for Crete and a happier time. It was a pity that in Rhodes, a delightful island which she had come to love, so much heartache had come her way.

She settled herself in the saloon of the steamer and tried

to concentrate on a novel, which she had bought at a kiosk. It was about Greece, and now she wished she had taken something else, one about Africa or Australia or Greenland. Later on, perhaps, she might be able to read about Greece and the islands when time had softened the pain of linking Greece with Mallory.

Someone stepped past her, then stopped. Some instinct warned her not to look up, but against her will, her better judgment, her head slowly lifted.

"I've come to take you home." Mallory spoke quietly, almost pleadingly.

Home! The word touched a sensitive chord within her, but she steeled herself against the urge to rise and fling herself into his arms.

"I'm not coming," she said. "You found you couldn't trust me. Why should I trust you? How am I to know when you'll fly into a rage and fling your accusations at me?"

"You won't know, because – oh, what does it matter?"

"It matters to me. If you really loved me, you'd trust me. You'd know that I couldn't willingly let you down."

"Come home with me, Jacynth. I can't explain it all here."

He lifted her by the elbows and she stood rigidly, her head turned away. Then, her will-power sapped, it seemed, she relaxed for a moment in his arms.

He held her close against him, then released her, picked up her suitcases and shepherded her out of the saloon and towards the gangway, just as a deckhand was untying the ropes. She thought woodenly that he had possessed her suitcases and she had little choice but to follow him.

His car was close by the quay and once inside, she sat up straight, her gaze fixed unseeingly ahead. Meticulously, she took care not to touch his sleeve when he swung round corners.

Contrary to her expectations, he remained completely silent until he opened the front door of the Villa Kalakos. Then he said, "Come into my study."

"I've chosen this room," he said when they were both

inside and he had, surprisingly, locked the door, "because this is where I came near to making the greatest mistake of my life."

"So even the great Mallory Brendon makes mistakes!" Jacynth taunted.

"What a shrewish vixen you'll become in a few years' time, if I don't take steps to tame you!" A smile lifted the corners of his mouth.

He planted her in his own armchair and remained standing. "First, I must take back every word of accusation I threw at you this morning."

"Thank you."

"I went to see Perandopoulos and he was most elated, not only at securing the contract, but because of his informant of our price."

Jacynth waited expectantly.

"Hermione came in then and I knew what her father meant when he said that blood was thicker than water. She told me that loyalty to her father was more important than to anyone else, including me. Unless, of course, the old man added, if I married his daughter, then all the secrets would be in the family."

"And did she tell you how she obtained the figures?" asked Jacynth.

"M'm. She said you were extremely careless – and let her in here to my study alone while she pretended to telephone me."

"I guessed that now, but how could I have stopped her? She was also in my office, glancing over the work in my typewriter. She was your friend – even the woman you might marry – what could I have done?"

Mallory came towards her and bent over her. "Nothing, against such a spiteful woman. She told me that she would never have used her information but for the fact that my engagement to you was announced – or rather, it spread through the bazaars, as it were."

With an effort, Jacynth rose, disengaged herself from

Mallory's hand. "Well, now that's been cleared up, perhaps I can leave again."

"For Crete?" he queried, refusing to let go her hand.

Then her face crumpled and the tears slowly coursed down her cheeks.

"Darling!" he whispered, taking her firmly into his arms and wiping away the tears. "I don't deserve your forgiveness, but I'm humbly asking for it. I was mad to doubt you. Jacynth, my love, please stay."

The entreaty in his voice finally broke her cold resolution and she clung to him, responsive at last to his gentle kisses, aware of the fierce, latent urgency of his desire and revelling in the ecstasy of that promise for the future.

After a long pause, Mallory asked, "And when do you leave for Crete?"

"Not tonight, apparently," she laughed.

"Nor tomorrow, nor ever – not without me," he threatened, his eyes shining with tenderness. "Together, we'll go places – and you shall see my country through the eyes of a bride."

She sighed and wound her arms round his neck. "Together," she murmured, "together. That's all I ever wanted."

romance is beautiful!

and Harlequin Reader Service is your passport to the Heart of Harlequin

Harlequin is the world's leading publisher of romantic fiction novels. If you enjoy the mystery and adventure of romance, then you will want to keep up to date on all of our new monthly releases—eight brand new Romances and four Harlequin Presents.

If you are interested in catching up on exciting and valuable back issues, Harlequin Reader Service offers a wide choice of best-selling novels reissued for your reading enjoyment.

If you want a truly jumbo read and a money-saving value, the Harlequin Omnibus offers three intriguing novels under one cover by one of your favorite authors.

To find out more about Harlequin, the following information will be your passport to the Heart of Harlequin.

the omnibus

A Great Idea! Three great romances by the same author, in one deluxe paperback volume.

A Great Value! Almost 600 pages of pure entertainment for only $1.95 per volume.

Essie Summers

Bride in Flight (#933)
...begins on the eve of Kirsty's wedding with the strange phone call that changed her life. Blindly, instinctively Kirsty ran — but even New Zealand wasn't far enough to avoid the complications that followed!

Postscript to Yesterday (#1119)
...Nicola was dirty, exasperated and a little bit frightened. She was in no shape after her amateur mechanics on the car to meet any man, let alone Forbes Westerfield. He was the man who had told her not to come.

Meet on My Ground (#1326)
...is the story of two people in love, separated by pride. Alastair Campbell had money and position — Sarah Macdonald was a girl with pride. But pride was no comfort to her at all after she'd let Alastair go!

Jean S. MacLeod

The Wolf of Heimra (#990)
...Fenella knew that in spite of her love for the island, she had no claim on Heimra yet — until an heir was born. These MacKails were so sure of themselves; they expected everything to come their way.

Summer Island (#1314)
...Cathie's return to Loch Arden was traumatic. She knew she was clinging to the past, refusing to let it go. But change was something you thought of happening in other places — never in your own beloved glen.

Slave of the Wind (#1339)
...Lesley's pleasure on homecoming and meeting the handsome stranger quickly changed to dismay when she discovered that he was Maxwell Croy — the man whose family once owned her home. And Maxwell was determined to get it back again.

Susan Barrie

Marry a Stranger (#1034)
... if she lived to be a hundred, Stacey knew she'd never be more violently in love than at this moment. But Edouard had told her bluntly that he would never fall in love with her!

Rose In the Bud (#1168)
... One thing Cathleen learned in Venice: it was highly important to be cautious when a man was a stranger and inhabited a world unfamiliar to her. The more charm he possessed, the more wary she should be!

The Marriage Wheel (#1311)
... Admittedly the job was unusual — lady chauffeur to Humphrey Lestrode; and admittedly Humphrey was high-handed and arrogant. Nevertheless Frederica was enjoying her work at Farthing Hall. Then along came her mother and beautiful sister, Rosaleen, to upset everything.

Violet Winspear

Beloved Tyrant (#1032)
... Monterey was a beautiful place to recuperate. Lyn's job was interesting. Everything, in fact, would have been perfect, Lyn Gilmore thought, if it hadn't been for the hateful Rick Corderas. He made her feel alive again!

Court of the Veils (#1267)
... In the lush plantation on the edge of the Sahara, Roslyn Brant tried very hard to remember her fiancé and her past. But the bitter, disillusioned Duane Hunter refused to believe that she ever was engaged to his cousin, Armand.

Palace of the Peacocks (#1318)
... Suddenly the island, this exotic place that so recently had given her sanctuary, seemed an unlucky place rather than a magical one. She must get away from the cold palace and its ghost — and especially from Ryk van Helden.

Isobel Chace

The Saffron Sky (#1250)
... set in a tiny village skirting the exotic Bangkok, Siam, the small, nervous Myfanwy Jones realizes her most cherished dream, adventure and romance in a far-off land. Two handsome men determine to marry her, but both have the same mysterious reason. ...

A Handful of Silver (#1306)
... in exciting Rio de Janeiro, city of endless beaches and skyscraper hotels, a battle of wits is waged between Madelaine Delahaye, Pilar Fernandez, the jealous fiancée of her childhood friend, and her handsome, treacherous cousin — Luis da Maestro. ...

The Damask Rose (#1334)
... Vicki Tremaine flies to the heady atmosphere of Damascus to meet Adam Templeton, fiancé of the rebellious Miriam. But alas, as time passes, Vicki only becomes more attracted to this young Englishman with the steel-like personality. ...

information please

**All the Exciting News from
Under the Harlequin Sun**

It costs you nothing to receive our news bulletins and
intriguing brochures. From our brand new releases to our
money-saving 3-in-1 omnibus and valuable best-selling
back titles, our information package is sure to be a hit.
Don't miss out on any of the exciting details. Send for
your Harlequin INFORMATION PLEASE package today.

**MAIL
COUPON
TO** Harlequin Reader Service,
M.P.O. Box 707,
Niagara Falls, New York 14302.

Canadian **SEND**
Residents **TO:** Harlequin Reader Service,
Stratford, Ont. N5A 6W4

Please send me the free Harlequin
Information Package

Name _____

Address _____

City _____

State/Prov. _____

Zip/Postal Code _____

ROM2011